The
SHAUGHNESSEY
ACCORD

The SHAUGHNESSEY ACCORD

ALISON KENT

BRAVA

KENSINGTON PUBLISHING CORP.
http://www.kensingtonbooks.com

BRAVA BOOKS are published by

Kensington Publishing Corp.
850 Third Avenue
New York, NY 10022

All Kensington titles, imprints and distributed lines are available at special quantity discounts for bulk purchases for sales promotion, premiums, fundraising, educational or institutional use.

Special book excerpts or customized printings can also be created to fit specific needs. For details, write or phone the office of the Kensington Special Sales Manager: Kensington Publishing Corp., 850 Third Avenue, New York, NY 10022. Attn. Special Sales Department. Phone: 1-800-221-2647.

Brava and the B logo Reg. U.S. Pat. & TM Off.

ISBN 0-7582-0670-4

First Kensington Trade Paperback Printing: November 2004
10 9 8 7 6 5 4 3 2 1

Printed in the United States of America

"With great power there must also come great responsibility!"
—*Introducing Spider-Man*

Amazing Fantasy #15, August 1962
Writer: Stan Lee
Artist: Steve Ditko

Original Price: $0.12
Near Mint Condition Price: $48,000

The
SHAUGHNESSEY ACCORD

One

The Smithson Group's Manhattan ops center, never a hotbed of mind-blowing excitement in and of itself, was duller these days than a plastic knife working at a stick of cold butter.

It was driving Tripp Shaughnessey out of his ever-loving gourd.

He understood the laid-back, uneventful, mellow-as-molasses mood; really, he did. But without something to do besides sitting and staring zombie-eyed at static surveillance feeds, he was at a huge risk for losing the rest of his mind.

The Smithson Group—Christian Bane specifically—had recently pulled the plug and sent Peter Deacon, the sleazy front man for the international crime syndicate Spectra IT, swirling down one nasty drain.

That only left, oh, another umpty dozen members of the organization to annihilate.

There were days it seemed nothing short of an apocalyptic, second-coming, end-of-world scenario would make a dent in the work the SG-5 team had remaining to do.

In the meantime, Tripp's eyes and ass needed a break. Even a highly trained Smithson Group operative could only sit and stare for so long without giving in to distraction.

He pushed up from a squat to his feet, righted his chair,

capped the tube of bearing grease he'd brought with him this morning, and tossed it to his desk.

He twirled the chair this way, twirled it that, sat and drew his knees to his chest.

Bracing the balls of his feet against the edge of his desktop, he shoved. The chair sailed into the center of the ops center's huge horseshoe-shaped workstation and beyond.

He was rolling, rolling, rolling . . . slowing, slowing, slowing . . .

"Crap."

He glanced to his right where Christian sat holding headphones to one ear, shaking his head.

He glanced to his left where Kelly John Beach faced him, arms crossed, brow arched.

Ooops.

"What the hell did I tell you? Inline-skate wheels, you maroon. Otherwise, forget it. You can't race Hot Wheels on a NASCAR track."

Tripp shrugged, leaned back in his chair, legs extended, ankles crossed. It was all good. He had it under control.

Laced hands behind his head, he stared up into the cavernous darkness of the twenty-fourth floor's ceiling that was nothing but a web of exposed ductwork.

"Thought I'd give the bearing grease a try before changing out the wheels. Picked the stuff up at a skate shop down in Philly last week."

His comment was met with snorting in stereo, and Kelly John's, "Waste of money."

Tripp rolled his eyes. "Now, how can you say that when I bested my record by ten feet at least?"

"Good to see you're keeping yourself busy," Christian said without looking up.

K.J., on the other hand, met Tripp's gaze straight on. "Yeah, don't you have some work to do?"

"Nag, nag, nag." Yes, he had work to do. Or he would as soon as the Spectra IT agent he had on his scope made a noticeable move.

The agent who'd chosen Brighton's Spuds & Subs Sandwich Shop at the end of the block as his base of operations.

Tripp hadn't yet made the dude's cover story; he only knew the agent was monitoring the early afternoon traffic coming and going from the building across the street, housing, among other things, a privately held, family-owned-and-for-the-most-part-operated diamond exchange.

Tripp was monitoring the traffic as well. Especially since it wasn't Spectra's MO to deal with such a small-time operation as Marian Diamonds—and because word on the street said Marian Diamonds was trading in illegal conflict stones smuggled out of Sierra Leone.

Sure, the Spectra agent could've been canvassing the dealings of the entire block—a lot of high dollar transactions went on in the financial district between the hours of nine and five.

But just about the same time Spectra had shown up at Brighton's, the grandson of Marian's owner had gotten a hankering for sandwiches eaten long past lunchtime, ordering corned beef and sauerkraut on rye to go the same time every afternoon.

Of course, his hankering could've been for Glory Brighton instead. In which case Tripp had a decision to make. Cement shoes or defenestration, because Glory Brighton was off-limits, whether she knew it or not.

His partners having put the kibosh on playtime, he spun his chair around and shoved off in the direction from which he'd come. This time he only made it two thirds of the way across the room.

Crap and a half.

He rolled his eyes. Christian chuckled. Kelly John offered up a round of applause and a suggestion. "Why don't you make yourself useful and go grab us some lunch?"

"I could. But I'm trying to keep a low profile here. Sticking with Hank's playbook and all that." Tripp followed the Smithson principal's instructions to the letter, but then so did all five of Hank's original handpicked operatives as well as the newest recruit.

Each one of them owed him, if not for the fact that their names weren't yet carved into nondescript tombstones, then for keeping them from a lot of years spent incarcerated at Leavenworth or Gitmo.

Besides, there was something about Hank's seventy-five years of experience at staying alive that spoke to a man.

"No one said you had to go to Brighton's," K.J. was saying. "Order a pizza. Pick up Chinese."

"Besides," Christian added, "there are other delis out there."

Tripp sputtered, feigning shock. "Heresy. Blasphemy. Other delis indeed."

K.J. waved Tripp away and turned back to the bank of monitors at his desk. "So, phone in an order. Have Glory leave it for you with Glenn in the garage. Pick it up there if you think your mark's gonna make you."

Tripp wasn't too keen on the idea. The garage separating the buildings housing Brighton's and Smithson Engineering—the cover for the SG-5 team—was no better than a war zone. The honking, the squealing tires, the exhaust fumes—not to mention the nosy punk parking attendant.

Forget getting in any quality Glory time with Glenn hovering around. And that quality time—even more than the freakish boredom—was the only reason Tripp was even considering venturing out of the ops center.

Kelly John and Christian might want food, but it wasn't too high on Tripp's list of priorities. He'd learned to do without in the weeks before Hank Smithson swooped down on salvation's wings and plucked him off a Colombian mountainside, and he'd never quite gotten back to his old way of thinking.

He ate enough to keep his body strong and able, his mind active and alert. Just not enough to start taking sustenance for granted. Not when he knew all too well the way life had of snatching away what he valued.

He glanced at the monitors on his desk. The first received the wireless feed from the camera hidden behind the marquee over the entrance to the Smithson building. He toggled left, toggled right. Nothing out of the ordinary on the street in front of Brighton's or the diamond exchange.

Next he glanced at the monitor showing the feed from Brighton's security system. Glory had no knowledge of SG-5's video tap of her wires. The shop's surveillance cameras were simply set up to encourage employee honesty, scare straight the kids working for her, stuff like that.

But they told Tripp what he needed to know. Spectra IT's agent had not yet arrived.

Tripp pounced on the window of opportunity, shooting out of his chair and making like a rabbit for the door to the safety vestibule. The walls of the tiny chamber were constructed of sixteen-inch steel and separated the SG-5 nerve center from the floor's areas of public access.

"Back in a flash," he said, pressing his thumb to the pad of the biometric sensor. Mechanized bolts and pins disengaged and the door swung open.

"Or at least in an hour or two," Christian corrected.

"Hey. A girl likes a guy who takes his time," Tripp said, stepping inside. The closing door cut off further contact, sealing him up like a hot dog in Tupperware.

Overhead lights switched on inside the high-ceilinged, four-walled enclosure outfitted top to bottom in soundproofing tile.

Funny about that. The soundproofing. The lack of outside contact. How it still got to him after all this time. The idea of help being within reach . . . but not.

It wasn't like he needed help, or that he was really cut off, as seconds later he punched the code and exited into the suite's bamboo and black-lacquer façade of a reception area. And the confining space wasn't an issue.

But the idea of being on his own sure was enough to cause a bitch of a hitch in his side.

"Fourteen-seventy-eight, seventy-nine, eighty, ninety, fifteen and twenty." Glory Brighton counted out her customer's change. "There ya go, Wes. And you enjoy that new baby girl, ya hear?"

"No worries there, Glory," Wes said, lifting the white bag containing sandwich and chips in a parting gesture. "See you tomorrow."

"Yep. Same bat time, same bat sandwich," she said, and Wes chuckled. Oh, yeah. She was absolutely hilarious. Really cracked herself up. Snort.

Glancing at the phone then just as quickly away, she shut the register drawer, straightened the stack of expensive tri-fold color brochures and take-out menus on one side, closed up the display case of freshly baked and individually cellophaned cookies on the other.

Two-twenty-five apiece, and people paid without thinking twice. And why should she complain? They cost her a fraction of that and made for quite the tidy profit.

She wasn't complaining. Just . . . having a bad day. No real reason she should be. Except for the fight she'd had on the phone with her mother this morning.

Which meant that her father, having gone home for his Thursday lunch of a meat loaf sandwich and potato pancakes made from last night's leftovers, and by now on his way back to the bank, would be calling before he sat down for the afternoon to review loan applications.

Your mother has your best interests at heart, Glory. She is thinking of your future. Her concern for your welfare shows how very much she loves you.

Nothing in there about Ann Brighton's dread at having to explain her only child's continuing lack of suitable matrimonial prospects to the ladies at the First Presbyterian Friday morning prayer circle.

The same group who two years later was still clucking over the fact that Glory had been taken in by that sweet-talking career criminal, Cody Scott, before he carjacked an undercover cop and got sent up the river to Riker's.

And nine months after the fact continued to sing a loud

chorus of hallelujahs that she'd learned the truth of Jason Piaggi's affiliation with the "Piaggi Family" before it was too late.

Even now Glory couldn't help but roll her eyes. Such drama over nothing.

Yes. She'd made two bad man choices in her twenty-seven years. A girl was allowed a relationship strike or two, wasn't she? Before being written off as a has-been?

"Hey, Glory."

She glanced to the right, down the long sandwich bar where Neal Baker stood rewrapping the ham he'd sliced up for Wes.

"Hey, Neal."

He grinned, but not at her so much as at their personalized "hey, you" routine. "You still need me to hang around while you inventory for tomorrow's order?"

Shoot. The order. She'd been so focused on the inevitable call from her father that she was on the verge of a screw-up bigger than her penchant for dating criminal losers.

She untied her apron, slipped it off over her head. She knew Neal's girlfriend's dance troupe's showcase premiered tomorrow night and tonight was the family-and-friends preview.

"Sorry, Neal. I'll make it quick."

"Mikki appreciates it in advance."

"She damn well better," Glory teased, grabbing her clipboard from beneath the counter.

She made a quick visual sweep of the shop, took in the customers still eating, and glanced at the pickle-shaped wall clock.

Nothing going on Neal couldn't handle alone. Hell, his efficiency made the lack of hers that much more obvious. Ugh. There she went again with the ridiculous self-deprecation.

She was plenty efficient, she mused, heading into the storeroom down the hall at the rear of the shop. Just look at the shelves in here. A place for everything. Everything in its place.

It was just the constant parental haranguing that enforced

the sense of being less. Less a good judge of character than expected of a daughter of Ann Brighton. Less respectable than what she would be as the married daughter of Milt.

And now with the trickle-down effect, she was feeling less efficient than her own part-time employee.

The only time lately she'd felt like *more* was when staring into the beautiful green eyes of one Smithson Engineering project consultant. That Tripp Shaughnessey. *Mmm-mmm-mmm.* Definitely one to throw a curve at a girl's plans.

Before he'd shown up in her shop weeks ago, months actually, though it seemed like days, seconds even, since she felt that first tingling rush of attraction every time he walked through her doors . . . before he'd shown up in her shop whenever it was, she'd been thinking of giving her parents' matchmaking efforts another chance, or two, or three.

Now she was thinking about nothing but having Tripp's babies. At least in a figurative sense.

Yes, she wanted to get married—eventually. Yes, she wanted to start her own family—when it was time. Yes, she wanted to test the proverbial boiling waters between Tripp and herself.

Right now, however, she needed to count the pickles so Neal could get going. The pickles, the olives, the paper napkins, the cans of tuna . . .

Could life possibly get any better than this? she mused.

And she was still musing ten minutes later when behind her the door to the storeroom slammed shut.

Two

Glory whirled around, hand pressed to the base of her throat. The click of the door latch still echoed as she stared at her intruder, glared at her intruder, watched as he reached down and turned the lock on the door, looking her way all the while.

Her gaze slid from his very large hand on the doorknob back to the face she saw every night in her dreams. She did her best not to sigh, to appear peeved rather than pleased, but it was hard when her tummy was tingling with blooming daffodil petals.

One eye narrowed, she pointed with the sharp end of her pencil. "You, Tripp Shaughnessey, are a very bad man."

"Ah, now, Glory, admit it. I'm not half as bad as you want me to be." He leaned his broad shoulders against the door, crossed his arms over his impressively buff chest, and grinned in that way he had.

That way that made her want to take off all of her clothes, piece by piece in a slow sultry striptease—a thought that sent the daffodil tingles tickling in deep dark places that seemed these days to have Tripp's name written all over them.

Returning her attention to the task at hand, she finished counting the gallon cans of black olives, marked her inventory sheet, then slipped the clipboard over the hook centered on the shelving unit's support rail.

It was time, she decided, once she'd filled her lungs with the air she needed to breathe. Time to put her plan into motion. Or to take it to the next level since she'd made the first move when she'd dressed this morning with Tripp specifically in mind.

She did that a lot these days.

"I dunno, Shaughnessey," she said, and turned. "I'm not sure any man has it in him to be that bad." She let her gaze crawl the length of his very fine body, smoothing her palms over the zipped-up and laced-up khaki miniskirt that hugged her hips and little more.

He took in the motion of her hands; heat flared in his bright green eyes. His thick honey-blond lashes came down slowly, lifted in another smooth upward sweep. His lips curved in a smile that said oodles about all the ways he knew to be bad.

It was the very look she'd been hoping for, had been waiting for, yes, had been planning for. She'd seen it—no, she'd *felt* it—so many times lately but never in the right place at the right time.

This, fingers crossed, could be both.

"Well, now. That sounds to me like a challenge," Tripp finally said after clearing his throat. He cocked his head to the side and considered her. "And here I thought you knew by now that I'm never one to back down."

She didn't know him at all. Not in the way she was determined to. In the way any woman would need to know the man she intended to become her intended as soon as she convinced him that he intended the same.

What she'd never counted on, however, was the sudden fluttering of nerves interfering with the daffodils and causing her to second-guess her brilliant master plan to seduce him, knock him senseless, leaving him desperate for more.

She thought of career criminals and mobsters and the First Presbyterian Friday morning prayer circle.

No. No second-guessing. It was now or never. She put her

foot down on all her doubts, fortified herself with another monstrous nerve-settling breath, and took a step toward him.

"It's hard to get to know a guy when he sends his friends for his lunch." One step closer.

"When he can't even be bothered to order his own turkey, avocado, sprouts and Dijon." Another step, and nearer still.

"Or when he comes at lunch rush, and a girl can't spare a minute to flirt properly."

Tripp pulled in a deep breath, blew it out with a shake of his head. "Oh, Glory. If you don't think what you've been doing is properly . . ."

"So you like?" she asked, tilting up her chin just the tiniest, flirtiest bit.

He growled deep in his chest. "I'd like it a whole lot better if you'd give improperly a try."

She grinned, laughed under her breath, pushed a hand back through her mop of black curls and decided she might be able to pull this off after all. "Thing is, Shaughnessey, for improperly I'm afraid I'm going to need a lot more help than you've been giving me."

His brow arched upward. He shifted his weight from one hip to the other. "That so?"

"Yeah. Definitely so."

She took her time closing the rest of the distance between them, not touching him, not quite yet, waiting for that, wanting to savor first contact. To press her lips to that dip in his collarbone and linger. To taste him. To breathe him in.

Her fingers itched to slip between the snaps of his pressed khaki shirt. Instead of following through, she glanced down and away from the pull of magic in his eyes. Her pink leather, wedged Mary Janes contrasted fiercely with his big bad, black motorcycle boots.

She was Red Riding Hood to his wolf. Little Miss Muffet to his spider. Wendy to his Peter Pan. He tempted her. He frightened her. She longed for him to sweep her away from the mundane and take her flying.

She was tired of making sandwiches and stuffing potatoes

and inventorying supplies for reorder. Tired of having no social life except that arranged by her matchmaking parents who were determined she make a sensible match.

Sensible, schmensible. She wanted romance.

Again she sighed, allowed her gaze—now a slight frown—to climb up his long denim-clad legs to that place beneath his Adam's apple still tempting her so. "You dress like no engineering project consultant I know of."

"You know a lot of us engineering types, do you? To know what we should be wearing?" He uncrossed his arms, hooked his thumbs through two of his belt loops.

The move drew her attention the length of his torso, that long, strong, lean body that she ached to cuddle up to more than anything she'd wanted in a very long time. When had she grown so tired and so needy and so very enamored of this man?

"Obviously my education is lacking in the engineer's wardrobe department." This time she circled one fingertip around his topmost snap, there beneath that spot she was crazy to kiss. "You're welcome to enlighten me."

"Fieldwork," he said simply, as if he wasn't sure of his voice. "Boots and jeans when on-site. Suits and ties for the office."

"I see." She liked him in both, liked the urbane sophisticate with his debonair flare, that cool James Bond detachment, that hint of a smoldering fire.

But it was the clothes he wore today that got to her, that gave her hope. He could very well have been the boy next door she'd grown up with, building forts and selling lemonade and practicing the art of French kissing.

He seemed less out of her league, more approachable.

And so she approached, her finger moving to toy with the next button in the long row down. "So you're off into the field? To consult on a project? Would you like a sandwich for the road?"

"Actually, I'm just back," he said, his chest rising and falling more rapidly now. "I thought I'd stop in and see what you had to offer."

"Well," she began, dampening her pressed lips with the tip of her tongue. "The turkey is always fresh, and I just set out a new Cajun baked ham and a roast beef seasoned with sea salt."

"Hmm." He widened his stance, adjusted his weight, balanced on both feet. "I was thinking of something sweeter."

"I don't believe that for a minute, Shaughnessey. You never order dessert," she replied, certain that she would soon be unable to breathe, having lifted her gaze to meet his.

The twelve-by-twelve cinder block room shrank to the size of a matchbox. It didn't matter that they were surrounded by industrial steel shelving and metal lockers and enough ketchup to paint the town red. All she knew was that bad boy look in Tripp Shaughnessey's eyes.

Forget the fairy tales. He was Tarzan, she was Jane, and the heat of the jungle seethed.

"Oh, I don't know." His voice was low, a raspy whisper, rough and achingly raw. "I could go for a mouthful of cake right about now."

When he set his hands at her hip bones, she let him pull her forward, inching closer with tiny, sliding, baby steps until their bodies were flush. Her fingers returned to the first snap she'd toyed with, the first in the long row down . . . and *pop*.

"I have key lime cheesecake." *Pop*. Her heart blipped in her chest like a target on a radar screen. "Italian cream cake." *Pop*. She curled her toes in her shoes. "Fudge pecan pie." *Pop*. Her fingers shook. "Butter brownies and chocolate chip cookies." *Pop*. Her lungs deflated.

She pulled the tails of his shirt from his waistband and pressed eight fingertips to the first ridge of muscle delineating his abs. "Do any of those sound good?"

"I'm not so big on sugar."

She resisted letting her fingers drift lower to see if he was big on her. Instead, she tested the resilience of skin and muscle from his abs upward, stopping only when she reached his collarbone. Then, her index fingers found and measured that sexy little indentation she'd dreamed of kissing.

Frowning, she tapped him there. "Lean down a minute. You've got something right here . . ."

He did. And she did. And he tasted like heaven.

Tripp froze, an ice cube under assault from a blowtorch. Oh, Glory. Hot barely began to describe her. And it sure as hell didn't make a dent in explaining the temperature of her mouth.

He flexed his fingers at her hips where he held her, loving the give of her flesh, the nicely rounded curves that filled his hands with no poking from protruding bones.

He'd come in here to surprise her, to tease her, to steal a kiss or two or three. Yet he was the one now scrambling to recover. The one wondering if recovering was what he wanted to do.

He cleared his throat and swallowed. As expected, Glory lifted her head, and he asked, "Did you find what you were looking for?"

Her eyes grew sleepy, dreamy, and she nodded. "I did, yes, thanks."

She dropped her gaze to his chest, slid her palms from his pecs to his shoulders. He slid his hands from her hips around to cup her fine rump and handfuls of thick khaki skirt.

A smile stole along the edges of her mouth. He took it as encouragement and tugged her forward into the cradle of his lower body. "Hope you don't mind. Just making sure you're comfortable."

She wiggled a bit. "What about you?"

Oh, he was hard and beginning to ache and thinking it had been a long time since he'd found relief with a woman who tickled his fancy and not just his— "I'm good. Comfy. Still thinking about dessert."

"Well, I do have a special recipe. One I rarely share." She kneaded his shoulders beneath his shirt.

Her hands . . . he groaned, liking that "rarely" part a lot more than made sense. "Yeah? What might that be?"

"It's fairly rich. Definitely sweet." Her fingertips drifted to his armpits, down the underside of his arms until his sleeves caused resistance. "I'd call it . . . intense. The way it feels when a lemon torte hits your tongue."

He knew the feeling. A sizzling burst of too much too soon, which quickly gave way to wanting more. With Glory, he wanted more. He wanted to linger.

How many licks did it take to get to the center—

"Tripp?"

"Glory?"

"You've changed your mind, haven't you?"

Her question was spoken softly, hesitantly, as if she were bracing for rejection when he'd given her no reason to. He had no intention of turning her down or of letting her down.

He just wasn't sure this was the time or the place.

"Are you kidding?" He shook his head to reassure her, gathered up more of her short skirt's fabric until his fingertips brushed the flesh beneath. He had a hell of a time swallowing his responding groan. "I was just thinking it might be nice to start with an appetizer."

"I think that's what we're doing," she said, looking up at him then from beneath a fringe of jet black lashes.

He chuckled. He liked that he hadn't scared her away. It was always a matter of balance, of taking his time as he tested the waters.

He gave a playful smack of his lips. "I'm not so sure. I'm not tasting anything here."

Her roaming fingers found the edges of his shirt, closed around the fabric, used his collar as a handle to pull his head down and press her mouth to his.

Three

She'd known by looking at his mouth that he'd be a wonderful kisser. She'd listened when he'd talked, watched the way he'd held his lips when considering what he wanted to order.

She'd known, but she hadn't known at all, because he kissed like Tripp and like no one else at all.

He was gently demanding, his hands having moved from her bottom to her head, the heels of his palms at her cheeks, his fingers threading into her hair as he held her.

Held her and kissed her as if she were the only woman in the world he wanted to kiss, the only one who mattered.

She loved the daffodil tingles sweeping through her body, loved the feel of his lips. The soft searching, the sweet nudging press as he urged her mouth open and slipped his tongue inside.

She released his shirt collar, moved her palms to his chest, enjoyed the dusting of hair there that tickled. He was lean, possessed with the type of body that seemed to thrive on less sustenance than more. Of that she was certain because of how little he ordered; she had often wondered how much of what he bought and paid for he actually ate.

His ribs lay beneath the same sleek muscle that rippled over his abdomen. She touched him there, explored all she could reach of his bare skin, setting loose a feral growl that rose in a rumbling wave from his belly up his throat.

His kiss grew demanding, grew hungry, as if what he needed right now in this moment were things only she had to offer. If he only knew how much there was, how deep ran her longing to give . . .

"Oh, Glory," he pulled his mouth free to mumble. "You amaze me."

"Why's that?" she mumbled right back, her lips brushing his cheek, his jaw, over his chin. "I'm not so amazing, really."

He chuckled. "Oh, yes. You are. Especially the way you do that. Right there."

"This?" she asked, her thumbs circling his navel like finely meshed gears. One clockwise, one counter, around and around and around.

He shuddered, clenched the muscles beneath her hands, nuzzled the skin under her jaw with his nose and his mouth, a little bit of teeth.

Heaven. Pure heaven. Absolute bliss. She couldn't conceive of anything better even knowing how much of the unknown remained to be discovered.

She slipped a hand around Tripp's waist, found the doorknob, made sure he'd turned the lock all the way . . .

The Verizon telephone panel van pulled into the alley behind the sandwich shop having made a final circle of the long city block.

The six men inside each wore identical black warm-up suits, athletic shoes, leather gloves and ski masks. All logos and labels had been stripped from the clothing, rendering each item as generic as was possible.

Each man carried the same Beretta 9mm. The guns no longer bore traceable serial numbers. None of them had ever been fired. Not in a crime, nor for fingerprinting by any firearms manufacturer. Not a single ballistics marking existed in any database.

The van had been jacked while the service tech took his

lunch break. He now lay blindfolded, gagged and trussed like a Butterball on the van's floor, but would be back on the clock in less than thirty minutes.

It would take the men half that long to get in and out of Brighton's though they'd been drilled to do it in less.

Danh Vuong wasn't the least bit worried about getting caught. He'd covered every base, taken every precaution. If anything came up, his men would adjust, improvise. They'd been drilled, too, to think on their feet.

No one working for Son Cam survived long without that particular skill, and Danh had been working for the man for close on twelve years now.

A dozen winters spent wearing Italian leather, cashmere and wool.

A dozen summers spent driving German luxury cars, riding in air-conditioned interiors behind bulletproof glass.

Danh was a far cry and a continent away from the stowaway wharf rat who'd made his way to the Los Angeles harbor via container ship, who'd crossed the grand ole U.S. of A. using his wits, his brains, his two hands and his mouth in ways a ten-year-old boy should never have had to do.

New York City had been his destination. No other location existed. He had plans. Big plans. And the past that had brought him here was now a very small memory. One he'd locked away and left to wither and die.

Danh double-checked the contents of his pockets. His cell phone was a prepaid throwaway he would use only should he run out of options. The zip ties would guarantee his safety as well as that of any bystander he was forced to restrain.

His contact at Marian Diamonds had gone mute, and had done so at the same time the Spectra IT syndicate had begun trespassing on Mr. Cam's business. It was an unsatisfactory state of affairs, one Danh intended to correct today.

During the last circle the van had made around the block, he'd seen the Spectra agent enter Brighton's. By the time the traffic signal at the corner had changed, the contact from Marian's had come and gone.

Danh was having none of it. Mr. Cam had given Danh a home when he had none, an education when he'd thought to never read, the food and clothing he'd wondered how to pay for.

He'd offered to pay in the same way he'd paid for his trip to New York from L.A. Mr. Cam had declined, teaching Danh his first real lesson.

With a family behind you, you were never on your own. Even if said family shared no blood but that which bound their oath.

Though Glory had double-checked the lock on the storeroom door, Tripp hesitated, uncertain whether she was keeping him in or keeping everyone else out. It was a subtle distinction that he doubted a lot of guys would make, but then, he overanalyzed on a regular basis.

That trait remained at odds with his tendency to take very little seriously, but it was the one that had drawn Hank Smithson's attention while the older man was busy boning up on the facts of Tripp's imminent court-martial—a future he himself had pondered while on the run from his own superiors in Colombia.

How Hank had gotten his hands on Tripp's *Top Secret* records remained a mystery the older man would take to his grave. Not a one of the SG-5 team members knew how or why he'd found and saved their sorry hides. Not a one of them really cared. The fact that he had was all that mattered.

Just like the fact that Glory had locked the storeroom door was all that mattered here.

Tripp moved his hands from her face, settled them on her shoulders, did his best to ignore the sensation of her fingertips flirting with his skin. It was hard when she flirted so sweetly, teasing him and tempting him there above his belt.

If he didn't ignore what was happening below, however, he'd be back at the ops center eating his lunch and wondering why the hell he hadn't savored this sweet opportunity to have dessert first.

Sweet. Oh, Glory. That's exactly what she was. Purely sweet. Her mouth, her fingers, her coffee-bright eyes when she looked up while brushing his collarbone with feather-light kisses.

He shuddered, kneaded her shoulders, whispered, "Amazing."

She chuckled, still kissing his chest and shaking her head. "Mandarin cream chocolate torte is amazing. Raspberry silk truffles rolled in powdered hazelnuts are amazing. I'm just Glory."

"You make my mouth water."

"That's what desserts are supposed to do."

He dropped his head back on the door and pulled in a breath he hoped would ground him back in the world of meat and potatoes. It wasn't happening. He was dying here. She was killing him sweetly, softly.

He'd stop if she said to. Only if she said to. But she didn't say a thing. One more deep breath and he pushed off the door, backed her into the wall at the right, spread her thighs with the knee he wedged between, and kissed her madly, feeling the thundering beat of her pulse where he cupped the base of her throat.

He sent his other hand exploring lower, down between their bodies to the hem of her skirt and her legs that he'd parted. He found her panties. Cotton. As soft as her kisses, as were the plump lips of her sex swollen beneath. He slipped a finger under the elastic at the crease of her leg.

She gasped into his mouth at the contact. He swallowed the sound, nudging his knuckle upward through her folds. Her fingers dug into his biceps. He feared she would push him away, that he'd gone too far, and readied himself to stop.

She pulled him closer instead, holding on while she whimpered, tipping her lower body upward, asking for the more that he so wanted to give her with body parts other than his fingers or thumb.

Time and place, man. Time and place.

He continued to kiss her, continued to play her, eating up her cries and whimpers the way he wanted to eat up the rest of her. He could taste the change in her, the salty electric tingle along her tongue, and knew she was close to coming.

He wanted to take her there, to give her this pleasure. She was so damn candy sweet, so vibrant, so open. It was a wonder he'd been able to keep his distance at all. He doubted he'd ever keep it again.

And here he'd been so good for so long, swearing off dessert, knowing how bad it was for him. But when Glory tore her mouth from his and whispered his name, when she closed her eyes and gave herself up to his touch, it was a surrender that knocked him breathless.

Her entire body shuddered; he felt her tremors where his limbs were tangled in and out of hers, where his torso held hers pinned to the wall, where his fingers eased her down from the high.

He watched her lashes flutter as she opened her eyes and slowly turned her head to look at him, watched her press her lips together, then bathe them with her tongue.

He pulled his hand from her panties, wishing he could linger and give her even more. But his pants were too tight and he had to get back to work and, ah, hell, a storeroom was no place to make serious love to this woman. Not in all the ways he wanted to.

She moved her hands up and pushed her thick mop of black curls from her face. She smiled then, as she looked at him and said, "Wow."

He grinned right back. "Good stuff, huh?"

She pulled in a deep, steadying, satisfied breath. "Lemon tortes have nothing on you, Shaughnessey."

He tossed back his head and laughed. This one was going to be a hell of a lot of fun to get to know better.

A hell of a lot of fun.

Danh ordered his men out of the van with no more than a wave of his hand. Footsteps fell soundlessly in the alley. The vehicle's doors closed without a creak. He waited for the five to fall in behind him, pressed to the building's wall, before he eased open the sandwich shop's back door.

He knew from earlier surveillance that they would be stepping into a small hallway that serviced the shop's restrooms and storeroom. The goal was to make it into the main shop undetected. Once there, phase two of the plan would be set into motion.

Right now, however, it was time to complete phase one.

He slipped through the door behind his number one man, Qua^n, standing guard while the other man checked both restrooms—empty—and the storeroom—locked—before blacking out the shop's security camera with spray paint.

Danh then signaled for the rest of his men to enter, left Qua^n at his post in the back hallway. He knew there were no scheduled deliveries the rest of the afternoon. Unscheduled, he had to cover for.

At his command, his four men spread out through the sandwich shop on catlike feet. Gasps and screams were cut off rapidly with a single wave of a weapon as Danh motioned the sole employee and five customers to gather at the rear of the shop.

Behind him, his men went to work lowering the blinds on the front windows, the ones covering the main door, the set hanging over the rear exit into the garage. The signs on both doors were turned to "Closed." The locks were secured as well.

Good. Done. Now to get what he had come for.

"Ladies and gentlemen, good afternoon. We will take no more than a few minutes of your time, then be on our way. If you will each stand and place your hands behind you, my men will secure both your safety and ours."

"Just take the money from the till and get the hell out of here."

Danh turned his attention to the young man wearing the name tag and the brown apron with Brighton's green-and-yellow logo. "If we were here for the money, Neal, we would be gone by now. Face the wall. Hands at your back. Everyone but you, sir, in the tweed sport coat."

Two of Danh's men quickly circled the hostages' wrists with zip ties. A third spaced out chairs against the side wall and settled their captives as comfortably as possible. The fourth of his men, along with Danh himself, ushered the Spectra agent into the shop's hallway.

Danh circled him slowly, taking in the costume of wool, cashmere and tweed, the ink-stained fingertips, the brown leather journal he still held tucked beneath his arm. The tiny gold-framed spectacles completed the picture, giving the agent the look of a scholar, a writer, the perfect cliché.

"Professor Shore, correct?" Danh queried, appreciating the brief flash of anger before the other man's features settled into an expression of fearful concern more appropriate to the situation.

The agent cleared his throat. "If you'll return the use of my hands, I'll gladly give you my money clip, my watch, anything you want."

Danh admired the man's absorption in his role. Spectra IT trained their agents well. "I am not interested in your money or your possessions, Professor. What I want is something that interests only you and I. Once you turn it over to me, I will release all of you and be on my way."

"You ain't going nowhere, dickhead."

Danh turned at the rudely shouted challenge and stepped back to view the customers lined up like a shooting gallery's ducks. "You, sir. You plan to stop me?"

"You bet your sweet bippy. Me and my brothers in blue. You've heard of New York's finest? I'm off duty." He indicated the phone hooked to his belt at his waist. "This baby's been transmitting to 9-1-1 since you and your Halloween parade started marching around."

Danh nodded to his nearest associate who removed the cell from the officer's belt and nodded. A sharp stirring of unease had Danh clamping down on saying more. After all, silence intimidated far greater than swagger. His temples throbbing, he simply inclined his head.

His man sent the hostage to the floor with a blow from the butt of his gun. The two female customers screamed, whimpered, sobbed. Danh's man acted automatically, quieting them both with duct tape before taking up his position again.

Ignoring the tic at the corner of his eye, Danh returned to his interrogation. Seconds later, a bullhorn outside sounded with a loud, "This is the police!"

The tic grew impossible to ignore. Now Danh was facing the only contingency he'd never planned for.

A standoff.

Four

"What the hell was that?" Tripp jerked his head away from Glory's and toward the storeroom's locked door. He stepped back while she smoothed down her shirt, adjusted her skirt and her panties.

Frowning, she followed the direction of his gaze. "It sounded like"—he pressed a silencing finger to his lips; she lowered her voice—"a police bullhorn."

"Yeah. That's what I was thinking." He held out a halting hand. "Stay where you are."

"Uh, okay," she said, agreeing like the good little girl who followed orders he obviously thought she was when what she really wanted to do was move the hell away from the one and only entrance into the room. "How long do you want me to stay?"

He didn't answer. Instead, he backed his way across the concrete floor, his gaze trained on the door until he reached the corner and the built-in, fireproof safety cabinet holding her safe, her files, and her security system's equipment.

She watched, mouth agape, as he twirled the dial on the cabinet's combination lock and opened the door. She was done standing still. "What the hell are you doing?"

"Shit. Your camera's down."

"What?" What the hell was going on here? "Look, Shaughnessey. You don't tell me how the hell you know my combination, not to mention where my monitor is . . ." She peered around his shoulder at the small television on top of the VCR recording the store camera's data.

He was wrong. The camera wasn't down. She could see movement in one corner. The rest of the lens had been blacked out by spray paint judging by the speckles peppering the missed spot. "I'm calling the cops."

"No," Tripp barked, but she'd already backed away and lifted the handset from the phone on the wall.

"It's dead." She held it out, away from her ear, wondering if the second line in the shop was still working.

Tripp nodded but kept his attention on the coaxial cable running into the back of the TV.

She hung up the useless phone, told herself she was in good hands, that she could trust him, even while a tiny voice reminded her that she didn't know him well enough to jump to that conclusion.

The things he was doing, the knife he'd pulled from his pocket, the fact that he was cutting into the cable . . .

She crossed the room, grabbed the wrist of the hand holding the knife, the hand he'd used to make her come, and stared him in the eye. "You tell me what's going on and tell me now or so help me—"

"What? So help you what? You'll run out the door into who knows what?" He pulled back the cable's black covering, shredded what looked like a coating of woven fabric around the core copper wire. "Stay put. That's all I'm asking."

She didn't want to do anything he said, not when he'd suddenly clammed up. Not when everything he was doing was as underhanded and sneaky—if not downright illegal—as anything that would bring out cops with bullhorns.

But staying put was what she ended up doing because she had no better idea. She looked on as Tripp twisted a short strip of the shredded fabric and tapped it against the copper. Three short taps, three long, three short.

An obvious SOS.

"Are you trying to signal the security company?" And why, with the police already outside? "I don't pay for twenty-four/seven monitoring. No one is going to hear that."

"They're not supposed to hear it."

Glory rubbed a hand to her tense forehead. This was getting worse by the second. "What, then? See it? How can they see it?"

"It's not your security service I'm trying to reach." He glanced sharply from the static on the blacked-out feed to the door, his brows drawn down into a deep V. "Can you take over? Three short, three long—"

"Three short. My degree might be in business, but I did learn your basic SOS."

"Good girl," he said.

She wanted to snap and growl at his use of "girl" but, quite frankly, she was too damned worried. Flat-out scared, if the truth be known, taking the cable from his hands.

Scared and suddenly longing for one of the safe-and-so-what-if-he's-boring dates of her parents' choosing. She wanted to be anywhere but here with this obviously dangerous man who turned her on, burned her up, then betrayed her by breaking into her not-so-secure security system.

She tapped the twisted fabric to the wire, felt a strange metallic tang in her teeth, wondered who the hell it was she was signaling. And, at the same time, sending out vibes to her mother's First Presbyterian prayer circle that she wasn't shorting out her only route of escape.

Sweat ran between Tripp's shoulder blades and pooled at the base of his spine. He'd been in such a hurry to get to Glory that he'd left his cell on his desk charging. Meaning, having it with him wouldn't have done him a fat lot of good anyway seeing as how it was dead.

He needed to reach the ops center, let Christian or Kelly John know something was going down. One of them ought to get hungry enough soon to realize he hadn't returned. Logic told him they'd check his monitor showing the Brighton feed, see the SOS static, and realize he had a situation here on his hands.

He trusted his partners to get him and Glory out. He trusted the cops out front to bungle whatever it was they were doing. Nothing particular against New York City's finest. His beef was with authority figures in general, letting power go to their heads, twisting the law to suit their purpose, lifting themselves above.

Sorta the way things had gone down in Colombia, leaving him facing the short stick of a court-martial for desertion—a way-the-hell-better scenario than sticking around to face certain death after blowing the whistle on the drug deals his superiors had been making in the name of the law.

With Glory looking on, not looking happy about what he'd asked her to do but at least looking like she wouldn't give up, he twisted the lock on the door as quietly as he could. Next, he turned the handle, cracked the door open and braced the bulk of his body for an inward attack.

Nothing.

His knife at the ready, he moved his head far enough to peer with one eye through the sliver of an opening, seeing nothing but the brown-and-yellow textured wallpaper and the edge of one of the shop's signature black-framed prints.

A centimeter wider, and this time the glimpse of black he caught belonged to what looked like the sleeve of a jacket. He shifted to his other eye, got nothing but the same perspective, and so cracked the door open further.

This time it was enough. He heard snuffling and whimpering and then an indistinctive voice—no accent, no inflection—calmly say, "Our friends outside are not going to deter me, Professor. I plan to be gone before they begin their textbook driven negotiation process to secure the safe release of our hostages."

Hostages! Shit!

"I would be more than happy to oblige"—this from a second, distinctly cultured voice—"if I had an inkling as to what you were talking about."

Tripp couldn't identify the players. The voices were unfamiliar. He had no clue as to what was happening. He only knew that he had to stop whatever it was.

The black sleeve shifted enough for him to see a slice of a head in a black ski mask. Again, no way to identify who or what he was up against without getting closer. He pushed the door closed without a sound, backed his way across the room to where Glory stood.

She stared at him, eyes wide and liquid though she hadn't shed a tear. She still held the cable he'd handed her, though at some point she'd stopped tapping out the SOS. It was good enough. One of his partners would eventually notice the problem with the Brighton feed.

Once they rewound the tape to find out when what had gone down, they'd devise a rescue plan in a hurry. But he couldn't wait around for any of that to happen. He wanted Glory safely out of here now. Even if he had to rely solely on himself.

He took the cable from her hands, moved her to the same spot she'd stood in before, before when he'd kissed her, when he'd made her come with his hand. "I want you out of sight in case anyone comes charging through the door."

"You want me to stay put, you mean."

"If something happens to you, I'll never forgive myself for not gorging on dessert when I had the chance."

She blinked hard to keep away the tears. "You are so not funny, Shaughnessey."

"No, but you're crazy about me anyway."

"Don't count on it."

"I've been counting on it for weeks already," he said with a wink. And then he sobered. "I need to find out what's happening. I don't want to put you in more danger than you already are, but I have to do this."

"Do what?" she pleaded in a whisper. "Why don't you just let the police handle it? I think we're safe. No one knows we're here."

"It won't take them five seconds to find out. I'd like to know who we're dealing with here should that happen."

"*We're* not dealing with anyone, Tripp. Please let the police handle it. This is what they're trained to do."

What was he going to tell her? That he didn't trust the police? That he was better trained than the good guys on the bullhorn but he wouldn't know about the bad guys until he took a closer look?

He finally asked her to simply, "Trust me? I'm not going to do anything stupid."

She gave him a look in return that said she wouldn't trust him half as far as Gary Sheffield could throw a baseball. So he held her fingers in his, brought them to his mouth and kissed her knuckles. Then he gave her a grin meant to tell her to leave all the worry to him.

He took his time cracking the door open again. The sleeve and ski mask obviously belonged to a lookout. The shop's back hallway was only accessible by those already in the shop or those using the alley's door. Meaning, whoever was making demands inside wanted new arrivals kept out and everyone else kept in place.

He took a deep breath, not sure if he was tamping down or revving up the adrenaline, nodded at Glory, and that was it. He pulled open the door. One long step into the hallway. A hand clamped over the guard's mouth. Pressure applied to a point just below his carotid.

The man was dead to the world from the choke hold before he even knew what hit him. And deader than deadweight as Tripp dragged him into the storeroom. Glory eased the door closed behind them. No more than a few seconds had passed. No real noise made. Tripp planted a knee in the small of the man's back.

He didn't bother with the ski mask yet but emptied all the

pockets, finding the two things he'd most wanted to find. A 9mm Beretta and a cell phone.

He tucked the gun into his waistband, punched a number into the phone that no government agency would ever be able to trace, and once connected said, "Shaughnessey."

Several minutes later, a computerized voice replied, "Thank you," signaling that his location had been made.

five

Once the biometric sensor read the scan of Julian Samms's thumbprint, the ops center's door slid open. He stepped out of the safety vestibule and into the cavernous room, the hub of SG-5's activities.

Christian and Kelly John both looked up. One nodded. One lifted a hand in greeting. Tripp wasn't anywhere to be seen. Eli McKenzie, the fifth member of the original team, had recently returned to the field in Mexico, having recovered from a nasty—and suspicious—poisoning.

"Where's Shaughnessey?" Julian asked, heading for his own desk to download the files he'd need in Miami where he was headed later today. Ostensibly to save a woman's life.

What he'd learned about her made him more ambivalent than was wise when prepping for a mission. But this one had tied herself to Spectra IT willingly, and he didn't have a lot of sympathy for anyone that dumb.

K.J. pushed away from his desk, swiveled his chair toward Tripp's corner of the workstation, and frowned. "He went for lunch. Like thirty minutes ago."

Typing his security code into the system, Julian snorted. "He go back to Philly for cheesesteaks, or what?"

This time it was Christian who pushed out of his chair. "He went to Brighton's. Check the feed. See if he's still over there messing with Glory. He did say something about taking his time."

The three Smithson operatives gathered in front of Tripp's desk, K.J. finally settling into the chair when it became clear that the camera broadcasting from Brighton's was broadcasting nothing but snow.

Julian and Christian watched as Kelly John checked the input and output connections, finding nothing wrong with the equipment, and queued the last thirty minutes of recorded feed to play.

"Jesus H. Christ." Christian picked up the phone on Tripp's desk five minutes later. "Hank needs to see this."

This being a blast of black spray paint out of nowhere followed by pulses of static that were an obvious SOS.

Christian dialed. Kelly John ground his jaw until it audibly popped. Julian switched to mentally cursing in Mandarin.

It was when the phone on the tracking computer buzzed across the room to signal a trace, that all three men turned.

And all three men started to sweat.

Hank Smithson stood in the wide triangle of space behind his desk and in front of his L-shaped credenza. His corner office on the twenty-third floor of the Manhattan financial district high-rise offered a view to beat all views.

He just wasn't in much of a mood to be viewing. Dad-blamed office work. He wanted to be back in Saratoga on the farm, watching MaddyB take a turn around the track, listening to the wind blowing down, and breathing in the smell of the Adirondacks.

Else he wanted to be upstairs, he mused wistfully, glancing toward the ceiling and wondering if he could get away with at least taking over a bit of the surveillance Tripp Shaughnessey was doing these days without his boys huffin' and puffin' about him needing to take it easy.

"Mr. Smithson?"

Easy was for wimps. Hank walked over to punch the intercom on his desk. "Yes, Emma?"

"I'm heading out for lunch. Can I bring you anything?"

Emma Webster. His secretary. Nope. Administrative assistant, she insisted on being called. A good woman. One of a very few he'd known in his life. "I'm fine. Ate too big of a breakfast this morning."

"If you're sure?"

"Yes, ma'am. I'm sure." He pictured the twitch of her perky nose. She hated to be called ma'am. "But, Emma? When you get back, will you find Jackson Briggs for me?"

"I'm sorry. Did I forget an appointment?"

He heard the fluster in her voice as she tried to recall any previous request he'd made for his chopper pilot's services. "Not at all. I was just thinking I might like to get back to the farm a couple days early is all."

"Let me get him for you now."

Hank shook his head, grinning to himself, thinking how much his Madelyn would've enjoyed Emma's dedication, the way she thought of everyone around her before ever thinking of herself. "You go on to lunch. Briggs will be around when you get back."

"Yes, sir. I'll be back in thirty minutes."

And she would be, too. The girl was always true to her word. He and Madelyn had never been blessed with children, but he would've enjoyed having a daughter like Emma.

Much as he could've seen himself as father to the five boys who made up the core of his Smithson Group, spending their days going where law-abiding, rule-stickling, by-the-bookers wouldn't and getting done what needed to get done.

Doing it all these days without him, of course, which grated on his nerves as much as the shrapnel he'd taken during Operation Just Cause in Panama continued to grate on his dad-blamed hip.

He needed to get out of here. He really did. He thought long and hard about ruining Emma's afternoon and raising Briggs himself while standing there, fiddling in his desktop humidor for one of his favorite Montecristo Corona Grandes, needing something to do.

And if that wasn't just the crux of it all, his needing something to do.

The thought was still on his mind, the wrapper still on his cigar, when the private line in the lower left desk drawer rang.

Tripp pocketed the cell phone that looked like a cheap throwaway without saying a word. He'd made a call but he hadn't spoken beyond saying his name.

Glory wasn't sure if she should start fuming now or wait for his lame excuses explaining away what looked like a lot of unlawful activity an engineering project consultant had no business engaging in.

Especially disconcerting was Tripp's way too familiar familiarity with the handgun he'd taken off the other man.

She watched now as he removed what she thought was called a clip, checked it for bullets before putting it back together and tucking it into his waistband beneath the right side of his shirt.

"Why not in the small of your back?" She gestured uselessly toward him. Uselessly because he wasn't even looking at her.

"Easier access on the side. Movies don't always get it right, you know."

No. She didn't know. And how the hell did he? "Just who the hell *are* you, Tripp? Or should I say, *what* are you?"

He did glance up then. "That's a conversation best had another time. Right now I need tape or twine or both. Whatever you've got back here to immobilize this one."

She had tape and twine both, found a roll and a spool in the same cabinet as her security system and handed them off. Tripp bound the man's hands and feet, pulled off his ski mask and taped his mouth.

"Anyone you know?" Tripp asked.

The young Asian didn't stand out at all in her mind, and she shook her head. "Do you still want me to send the SOS?"

Tripp dragged the unconscious man to the center of the

room. "No. If they were going to pick up the signal, they would've done so by now."

"Who are *they*?"

"Friends of mine." He returned to the door.

She glanced down at the other man, a kid, really, lying between them. "Don't you want him out of the way?"

"I want him where he can't kick over any of your shelves if he wakes up while I'm otherwise occupied."

"Occupied doing what, exactly?" She hated feeling left out when she was up to her eyeballs involved. "It would be nice if you'd let me in on what's going on here seeing as how this is my shop and all."

"Glory, sweetheart. I swear I'll tell you everything. Just not right now."

"So, I stay put." Ugh, but that grated. Not that she would have a clue how to get herself out if he wasn't here.

"Staying put would be great, thanks."

She felt useless, worthless, scared in so many ways she was numb with it. But she still had to fight the urge to stick out her tongue at his back. "Okay, but do you have a plan? What do I need to do while you're doing whatever it is you're doing?"

She heard Tripp sigh, but it wasn't a sound of exasperation. More like a sound of patient resignation. He glanced at her, admiration warming his eyes. Seeming to register all of what she was feeling, he moved from the door to cup her face in his hands.

"I'm sorry. I wish like hell this wasn't happening, that you weren't having to go through this. I'm operating here on autopilot, and I'm not used to making explanations. I need you to trust me."

Autopilot? Explanations? She focused on the one crazy truth that she knew. "I do trust you. What do you want me to do?"

"Oh, Glory." He tickled her with a teasing laugh. "If you only knew."

"Try me."

His gaze heated possessively. "I intend to, in every way possible. As often as possible." He let that sink in a simmering moment before adding, "After you're safe."

Too late, Glory thought. *I'm already a goner.*

After a long moment, one tense with all the things unspoken between them, he lowered his hands and took a step back. "It's not a big deal, really. Just my military training rearing its ugly head."

"You were in the military? Before Smithson Engineering?" There were so many things about him she didn't know, wanted to learn, wondered if she'd ever have the chance.

He nodded. "Same route a lot of guys take when they're clueless as to their future."

He said it blithely enough that she didn't believe anything about Tripp Shaughnessey's years in the military were the same ole, same ole at all. "You were Special Forces, right?"

He twisted his mouth, a cockeyed smile that answered her plain as day. "What makes you think that?"

It wasn't about anything he'd done. Simply about who he was. "Because I can't see you settling for less than being the center of attention."

"Ah, but that's the thing about Special Ops." He leaned forward, kissed the tip of her nose. "We're not supposed to draw any attention."

"I knew it. I was right."

He conceded nothing. Only cupped her cheek, rubbed a thumb along her cheekbone. "Does that mean you're going to trust me now?"

"Stay put, you mean."

"It's nothing but semantics, sweetheart. Nothing but that."

Danh paced the length of the service counter, staring at the meats, cheeses, sauces and vegetables though what he saw instead was the disappointment on Mr. Cam's face.

This was a simple operation. He had prepared for all contingencies. Having an off-duty police officer in the shop at the time of his plan's execution should have made no difference at all.

His men were highly trained. The fact that the two assigned to secure the customers hadn't seen the call made to 9-1-1 troubled him. He had failed in their training, and now all six of them were in danger.

The sandwich shop's telephone began ringing. The police making contact, determining his demands, seeing to the state of the hostages. Was anyone hurt? Would he release any women he held? Could they talk to one of the hostages?

Soon the proper authorities would be called and the necessary technical experts gathered to cut off the shop's electricity. Whether this happened before or after negotiators were brought in would be based on Danh's intent to cooperate.

Danh, of course, had no such intent at all.

He would not betray Mr. Cam. He and all his men knew that death was a possibility at any time. Today could as easily be the day as tomorrow.

The ringing of the phone finally ceased. The bullhorn started up again, as did sniffling from the two women customers who had been dining together. He needed the hostages out of the way and caught the gaze of one of his men while gesturing encompassingly. "Take the hostages into the back hallway."

The sniffling increased and was accompanied by whimpers. Danh paid no attention until one of his men ran back into the shop and called, *"O dau, Qua^n?"*

Danh's head came up sharply, an animal sensing a predator. Qua^n had been posted as lookout. He would never have left his post willingly. Meaning . . .

Danh headed into the back hallway. He tried the alley door. It remained locked from the inside. Both restrooms remained empty. Leaving no other option but the storeroom locked from the inside.

He shook his head slowly, allowing peace to settle over him. And then he reached for his gun and fired.

Six

"Fuckin' shit on a stick."

Tripp grabbed Glory by the shoulders, twirled her bodily across the room and into a tight corner where two of the shelving units met at a right angle.

"I know this part," she whispered as he wedged her inside. "Stay put."

He nodded, drew his gun, pressed his back to the wall at her side. The door slammed open, bounced off the cinder blocks behind. Tripp held the weapon raised, both hands at the ready, his heart doing a freight train in his chest.

Beside him, Glory barely breathed. The shelf of supplies to his right blocked his view of the door but didn't keep his nostrils from flaring, his neck hairs from bristling, his adrenaline from pumping like gasoline.

He sensed their visitor long before the black-garbed man swung around and aimed his gun straight at Glory's head. The intruder stepped over his own downed associate and held out a gloved hand.

"Give me the gun and she will not die."

Tripp cursed violently under his breath, weighing his options on a different scale than he would've used in this situation had Glory not been involved.

If he'd had time to do more than react, time to think, plot

and plan, he would've stashed the gun behind a can of olives and used the butt end to up his own prisoner count when the time was right.

Instead, he found himself surrendering the very piece that would've gone a long way to protecting Glory from this thug. Now he was stuck using nothing but the wits that never seemed to operate at full throttle unless he had a contingency plan.

Right now all he had was a gut full of bile. That and a big fat regret that he didn't think better on his feet than he did.

Having passed off the gun, he raised both hands, palms out. "Let's neither of us go off half-cocked here."

The other man considered him for a long, strange moment, his black eyes broadcasting zero emotion while he stared for what seemed like forever before he tugged the ski mask from his head.

He was young. Tripp would've guessed twenty-three, twenty-four. Except when he looked at the kid's eyes. His expression was so dark, so blank, so unfeeling it was like looking at a long-dead corpse.

Without moving his gaze from Tripp's, the kid shouted sharp orders in Vietnamese. Two other similarly garbed goons entered the storeroom and dragged away the deadweight Tripp had left in the middle of the floor.

Once the cast of extras was gone, the lead player planted his feet and shifted his gaze between Tripp and Glory, both hands hanging at his sides, one worrying the ski mask into a black fabric ball, the other flexed and ready and holding the gun.

"An interesting situation we find ourselves in here, isn't it?" he finally asked. "Miss Brighton, would you introduce me to your friend?"

"What do you want?" she asked before Tripp could stop her. "Tell me what you want. I'll give it to you, and you can get out of my shop."

His black hair fell over his brow. "If what I have come for

was so easily obtained, then I would have it in my possession by now."

He was after whatever the courier from the diamond exchange had delivered to the Spectra agent. Tripp was sure of it. Was sure as well the information would detail future packets removed from Sierra Leone.

The ski mask fell to the floor. "I'm waiting, Miss Brighton."

"He's a friend. A customer." Her hands fluttered at her waist. "We're just . . . good friends."

"You allow all your customers to visit your storeroom?" His mouth twisted cruelly. "Or only the ones with whom you are intimate?"

Glory gasped. Tripp placed his arm in front of her, a protective barrier he knew did little good. "C'mon, man. There's no need to go there."

The Asian kid raised a brow. "Actually, I think there is. Getting what I want often requires me to explore a defense's most vulnerable link. It is not always pleasant, but it can be quite effective."

Tripp was pissed and rapidly getting more so. "Well, there are no links here to explore. So do as the lady suggested. Take what you've come for and let us all get back to our lives."

"Were it only so simple," he said as he gestured Glory forward. She forced her way past the barricade of Tripp's arm. "But we seem to have hit what will no doubt be an endlessly long impasse thanks to one of Miss Brighton's customers."

Glory looked from the kid back to Tripp, her eyes asking questions to which he had zero answers. "I don't understand."

"You are very predictable, Miss Brighton. As is your customer base. Same sandwiches. Same lunch hours. That made planning this job quite easy. I'm assuming the courier using your place of business for a drop point found your tight schedule advantageous, too."

Tripp's mind raced like the wind. The kid was talking way too much. His gang had blacked out the shop's single security camera, had made entry without alerting anyone to their pres-

ence, had secured the scene and done it all while Tripp made
love to Glory.

Fuckin' shit on a stick barely covered it. He'd been monitoring the shop for weeks and he'd never noticed the place
being scouted. He hadn't been wise to the entire intrusion until
the police bullhorn had sounded outside.

A guy who followed through on such flawless planning didn't
start yapping his flap unless he felt there would be no sur-
vivors but him. And Tripp had a feeling they were looking into
the eyes of an animal who'd fight to the death before being
taken alive.

"I'm sorry," Glory was saying. Tripp heard the tears in her
voice. "I really have no idea what you're talking about or
what you want."

She stood in the center of the room where minutes before
the downed man had lain. The kid walked in a circle around
her, clearly agitated now. An agitation that had sweat gather-
ing in Tripp's armpits.

He didn't like the look that had come into the other man's
eyes or the tic twitching in the vein at his temple. It was a look
that shimmered with the need for revenge. An ugly need. An
ugly revenge.

"Listen," Tripp started, cut off by the kid's sharply spoken,
"Do not speak," which was followed by instructions called
through the door in his own language. Seconds later, another
man appeared and, on orders, approached. "Turn around.
Hands behind your back."

Now Tripp was beyond being pissed off. Especially when,
at his hesitation, the kid pressed the gun barrel to Glory's
head. His palms slick with sweat, Tripp turned and stared
blindly at the storeroom's cinder block wall. Blindly, because
all he saw was Glory's terrified expression.

That solid reality, her fear, was what he needed to keep
forefront in his mind. This wasn't a mission where he had others watching his back. This was a solo run. This was about her

life. And he knew she had a lot better chance of coming out of this in one piece with him keeping his head.

The thug at his back bound Tripp's hands together with a zip tie that came close to cutting off his circulation. He bit down hard on his anger and turned around, maintaining as passive an expression as his temper allowed while the kid's henchman patted him down.

Once the third man was gone, Tripp asked, "Now what?"

"Now you tell me your name."

Unless undercover or disguised, all the Smithson operatives existed in the private sector as the engineering project consultants they were. "Shaughnessey."

The kid nodded. "My name is Danh Vuong. I find negotiations so much more effective when personalized. Does that make sense to you Mr. Shaughnessey? Miss Brighton?"

Tripp nodded without agreement, wishing Julian Samms were here. Julian could read people as if they were printed on paper. Tripp had only his instincts to work from.

And those instincts were screaming at him to put this kid down. The way he was pacing and circling Glory. The way his forehead beneath his shock of black hair had beaded with sweat. He was on his way to careening out of control.

Tripp needed to draw the other man's attention away from Glory and onto himself without blowing his civilian cover. "It's tough to negotiate anything when we don't know what it is you want."

"What I want is something Miss Brighton is going to help me get." Vuong looked from Tripp to Glory. Or, more precisely, he looked at Glory's breasts where her chest rose and fell beneath the ribbed knit of her tank top.

The fabric was a pale pink and it hugged her body the way any man liked to see a tight tank top do. Zippers that matched those on her skirt decorated both shoulder straps.

With Tripp looking on, Vuong flipped one of the zipper pulls up and down using his gun barrel's tip.

Glory literally threatened to shake out of her shoes.

"Dude, hey. Would you get the gun out of the lady's face?" Tripp surged forward, purposefully awkward—only to have the Beretta shoved against his Adam's apple until he choked.

He continued to cough and gag as Vuong backed him into the wall. "You, Mr. Shaughnessey, are on the verge of becoming my biggest liability to date. Don't move. Don't speak unless you are spoken to. I would hate to mar this operation by killing you, but I won't hesitate if you give me reason."

Giving the kid reason would mean endangering Glory further. Tripp had yet to meet a killer who had qualms about removing all human roadblocks to his goal.

Once Vuong released him, Tripp dipped his head, working to clear what felt like a permanent constriction in his throat. He watched the kid return to Glory and this time run the gun barrel underneath the curves of both her breasts.

Her nipples tightened, a response to the stimulation that was all about the same fear widening her eyes.

"Very nice." Vuong moved the gun barrel higher, circling one of the taut peaks now pressing through both bra and tank top. "Very nice. Tell me, Mr. Shaughnessey. Does she respond this nicely to your touch? Or is she only turned on by the idea of losing her life?"

Fucking bastard. Talking about Glory as if she didn't exist. Still, Tripp didn't say a word. He'd been spoken to, asked a direct question. It didn't matter. His voice was stuck in his damaged throat, his words battling in his head to be heard.

Vuong turned his gaze in Tripp's direction. "Feel free to answer, Mr. Shaughnessey. In fact, I insist."

Tripp cleared his throat with a grunting sort of cough. "That's fear, man. Not arousal."

Vuong nodded thoughtfully, his eyes waking from the dead. "Our bodies are so complicated, yes? Yours, for example, is as tight as a wenched cable unloading cargo from a ship. While mine is . . . what do you think, Miss Brighton?"

"About what?" she asked softly, her voice steadier than Tripp would have thought.

But that was probably because he was back on the strange idea of a cable unloading a cargo ship. A background piece he filed away.

"About my body language. What emotion am I broadcasting?"

When Glory raised a brow uncertainly, he nodded once. Whatever the intent of the other man's question, Tripp wanted to see Vuong's reaction to Glory's response.

"Uh, I think you might be a bit nervous or upset since things haven't gone the way you were expecting."

Vuong silently considered her words before stepping close enough to drag the gun barrel along the waistband of her skirt. She gasped, trembled. Tripp seethed, steam bellowing from his nostrils, but he stayed where he was.

He needed to get to the knife he'd left with the security equipment after cutting into the coaxial cable. To do that, he needed the bastard out of the room.

But launching himself forward and driving his shoulder into Vuong's gut wasn't the way to get it done.

"She is right, you know, Mr. Shaughnessey." Vuong had obviously sensed Tripp's barely controlled fury since he swung the gun toward him in warning. "At least about me being upset. But then, who wouldn't be after having a plan foiled by an unforeseen circumstance."

"What circumstance?" Glory whispered.

Vuong glanced back at her face before dropping his gaze the length of her body and nuzzling the gun along the zippered fly of her skirt.

"One of your customers. An off-duty police officer managed to dial 9-1-1 on his cell phone and leave the connection open as we were seeing to his safety. Had he simply left well enough alone, we would've been long on our way."

Glory nodded. Tripp waited. Vuong pressed his body into Glory's side and slipped his gun hand beneath her skirt.

"I hate John Waynes," he said as tears rolled silently down her cheeks.

Tripp's gut knotted with the furious boiling of his blood.

He twisted his wrists this way and that, shifted a step to the side and fingered the shelving, looking for an edge or protruding bolt sharp enough to saw through his bonds.

"I came to this country when I was ten years old," Vuong was saying. "I naively thought cowboys still roamed the land and rescued innocent victims. I expected justice. But the world is not about justice, is it Miss Brighton?"

Glory looked at Tripp for help, her expression transmitting everything she felt. That if she said anything wrong, the gun beneath her skirt would explode.

He hadn't been spoken to, so not speaking seemed the wisest move. It also seemed like a cowardly one, when everything inside him screamed that he should roar like a lion and deal with the fallout that came.

And so he mouthed the only thing he thought might help. The only words that he knew she'd be able to read from his lips: *I love you.*

The shaky smile at the corner of her mouth bloomed in her eyes. He doubted she believed him, but at least he'd given her hope.

"Justice, Miss Brighton?"

"It should be," she said tentatively. "But, you're right. Too often it's not."

Vuong moved around behind her then and her sigh of relief filled Tripp's lungs. He wasn't even aware he'd forgotten to breathe.

"You're wrong, Miss Brighton. The world is as it should be. It's all about loyalty. Loyalty and suffering."

Glory shook her head. "I don't understand."

Tripp didn't understand either. That didn't stop him from tuning in with his antennae zinging. Or from slowly continuing to rub the zip tie along the edge of the shelving unit that had already drawn his wrist's blood.

"Your customer was loyal to his profession. I admire that. But because of that, he will suffer. I, too, must be loyal to my employer." He stood behind her now and wrapped his arm around her waist.

The arm with the hand still holding the gun. "Even if my loyalty causes suffering as well."

And then he slipped his free hand beneath Glory's skirt and reached between her legs.

Seven

Glory froze. She wanted to bolt, to scream, to spin around and knock the shit out of the man at her back. But he held her too tightly, he had a gun, and Tripp had told her he loved her.

So she froze.

Tripp didn't really love her. What he was doing was keeping her spirits up. Distracting her from the fact that the gangster holding her shop under siege was now feeling up her ass.

Violation was a term she'd never thought of in personal terms. It was more about library fines, ignoring an expiration date when the milk still tasted good. It was about crossing the street on red. About pulling tags off of mattresses.

Now she understood the difference. And she wanted to curl into a fetal position and die.

Only the look on Tripp's face kept her upright. A look that told her this other man's touch wasn't about sex but about control, about power. A brow daring her to defy his certainty that she could handle anything. A set of jaws that ordered her to hold on, to be strong.

She lifted her chin. He nodded his approval. And then she did the unthinkable. She issued her own challenge to the man at her back by spreading her legs.

He released her almost immediately, walked around her as if considering whether to shoot her or slap her down. Before he could do either, the police bullhorn sounded. The shop's phone began to ring. A second later, one of his men called out.

A break in the impasse. She wanted to weep with joy.

"You'll have to excuse me, Miss Brighton. It seems I have business to take care of."

Glory didn't even nod. She simply closed her eyes while he secured her hands behind her as Tripp's were secured. When Danh walked out of the storeroom, he even had the courtesy to close the door.

It wasn't like they could keep him from coming back, considering he'd shot the lock off.

Silence descended. She'd never before realized how nearly soundproof this room really was. All she could hear was her heart beating out *you're alive, you're alive.*

She opened her eyes then and met Tripp's bright gaze, starting forward, wanting to throw her arms around him more than she wanted to breathe.

But all she could do was lean into his body as he leaned into the wall, tuck her face into the cradle of his shoulder, and swear to get her hands on him at the earliest possibility.

"What the hell is happening? Oh, God, I thought I was going to be sick." Even now she feared hyperventilation. "Who is this freak?"

Tripp nuzzled his chin to the top of her head. "I'm not sure, sweetheart. He's a pro, whoever he is."

"This is insane. What could he possibly be looking for here?" She listened to the slight scratch of his midday beard against her hair, to the drumbeat of his heart beneath her cheek.

"I don't think it's about the shop. I think it's about him wanting something someone out there has."

"One of the customers? The cop?" Who had she seen after she'd rang up Wes's order and before she'd come in here to count olives?

The two secretaries from the investment firm on the next block who took a late lunch every day. The professor writing his memoir who always sat near the front window. The off-duty cop she didn't know. The driver for the *Post* who usually came in on Thursdays.

Tripp shook his head. "No. Not the cop."

And how would he know...? She stepped back far enough to look him straight in the eye. "You know who it is, don't you?"

When he didn't respond either to confirm or deny, she pressed harder. "You know who it is the same way you knew someone would see the SOS you tapped out on that cable."

Again with the blankly uncommitted look.

"Dammit, Shaughnessey. You'd better start talking and now."

"You're safer not knowing."

"Safer?" Was he crazy? "Are you out of your mind? I've had a gun to my head, to my chest, and up my skirt. You call that safer?"

"Safer than being dead."

"Who's to say that's not next on our Mr. Vuong's agenda?"

Tripp's silence was answer enough.

"Please, Tripp. If I'm going to die, I'd like to know the reason."

"I'll feel better about telling you once my hands are free."

A weird response. At least it wasn't a no—though once she wiggled her wrists against her own bonds she realized it might as well have been. "Is there a trick to getting out of these things?"

"Yeah." He nodded toward the storage cabinet. "My knife. If I get it down, you think you can cut through this plastic without slicing off my hands?"

"As long as you return the favor."

He grinned at that, buzzed her cheek with a kiss as he headed for the storage cabinet, visually measuring the distance to the shelf where he'd left his knife and coming up short.

Or at least short for a man who wasn't a double-jointed circus act. He only needed another foot at the most ...

"Here," she said, toeing a gallon can of jalapeño peppers off the bottom of the nearest shelf and sliding it across the concrete floor.

Tripp stepped up, stretched up . . . "Shit. I need another six inches."

"I wouldn't be saying that to just any girl if I were you."

He glared down at her. "Making funnies in the face of death, are we?"

A shiver turned her spine to jelly. "Do you think we're going to die?"

"No, Glory. We're going to live to tell our grandkids about this." He hopped down, glanced around the storeroom.

"Here. Let me try." She was shorter than he was but knew from watching his attempt that she had a more flexible range of motion.

Unfortunately, she would need five-foot arms to reach. She hopped back down. "Crud. Wait. Shove that crate over."

The plastic box in the room's far back corner held napkins and sandwich bags imprinted with her old logo. Tripp shoved and kicked it into place and climbed up.

The extra height was enough. He grabbed around, his hand smacking the shelf, the wiring, the TV screen, and finally the knife.

He jumped down, scooted the crate back into place while she closed the cabinet doors. He then ordered her to, "Back up. I'll cut you free first."

She did, reaching for his fingers that were warm and reassuring and then suddenly not there. She looked back over her shoulder. Then turned all the way around. "Tripp?"

He was mentally in another time zone, standing there shaking his head. "I'm not so sure."

What! She literally stomped her foot. "Dammit, Shaughnessey. What're you waiting for?"

"For a time when we need the upper hand."

"We need it now!" she wailed.

He shook his head. He'd turned into this robotic machine.

Thinking, not feeling. "We'll need it later more than we need it now."

"Later? I don't want to be here later. I want to get out of here now."

The only sound she heard in response was the click as he closed up the knife.

"Tripp," she whined, begged, entreated. "Don't do this to me, please?"

But he ignored her and her pleas, his gaze canvassing the room at hip level as he searched for a place to stash the knife. An easily accessible place for the "later" when he expected to need it.

That place turned out to be an open box of Advil packets she provided for her employees. The lip of the box slanted at enough of an angle to hide the contents. The knife disappeared beneath the plastic squares of white and peacock blue.

Now it was her turn to snag his attention. She approached until she stood full in his face, then approached further, backing him into the wall as she spoke. "If you don't tell me who the hell you are and what the hell is going on, I'll use that knife on you myself."

A grin spread over his mouth, easing the tense lines into which he'd set his jaw. But the tendons in his neck did not relax. And his eyes remained strangely distant.

"You promised," she goaded when still he didn't speak.

"I'm not so sure I promised," he hedged.

"You told me you'd tell me what you thought was going on here. So I wouldn't go to my grave wondering."

"I should've let you cut me free."

"Change of heart?"

"Yeah." He sighed heavily. "I'd really like to hold you."

"Oh, Tripp." The sting of tears threatened to blind her. She pressed herself to him; he was the one solid thing in the room that gave her hope.

"I'm not going to let you go to your grave, Glory." He paused, she waited, the punch line came. "Not till I've gotten mine."

She shook her head. His chest beneath her cheek vibrated with his chuckle when she stuck out her tongue. "Blackmail works both ways, you know."

"That's what I was afraid of. Besides, I was lying. I'm not going to let you die whether I get in your pants again or not. I'm not going to let anything happen to either of us."

The segue was perfect. "You sound pretty confident there for an engineering project consultant."

"Yeah, well, that's the thing. Besides the military back-ground, I have a lot of other, uh, outside training."

Her ears perked up, as did her intuition, which told her this armed forces thing was something Tripp rarely talked about. That he hesitated telling her even now—and wouldn't have if not for this anomalic situation in which they found them-selves.

"What sort of training?" she prodded when it became obvi-ous he thought he was done. As if she was going to let him off that easily.

"You think we can sit?" he asked, distracting her again.

"Saving your strength along with the knife?"

"Something like that," he answered and slid down the wall to sit, knees bent and spread.

She settled between, leaning her shoulder into his chest and giving herself the visual advantage of being able to look into his eyes.

She wanted to make sure he didn't try to pull anything over on her. Like some big fat lie of a story to make her feel better, hoping she'd forget that in the next moment they both might die.

Eight

Figuring out how much to say about who he was and what he did had never come easy to Tripp. Keeping the existence of SG-5 off the public radar was essential. Keeping it off all military and law enforcement scopes was paramount.

The Smithson Group righted a lot of wrongs bound up in legal red tape along with others that went largely ignored for a variety of political reasons.

SG-5 wouldn't be able to guarantee many happy endings with Big Brother breathing down its back. But if this siege was indeed Glory's Last Stand, he owed her as much of the truth as he could reasonably share.

So when she prodded him with a softly uttered, "Tripp?" he shrugged, and said, "It's no big deal really."

And then she butted him with her shoulder. "You are so full of crap."

A firecracker. A pistol. She was one of a kind and made it really hard for him not to smile. "Now, what makes you say that? You have your own training to compare what's a big deal and what isn't?"

"No, but if you're relying on basic stuff, then Brighton's is a kosher deli."

She wasn't going to let him bullshit his way out of anything, was she, perceptive little wench. "Hmm. I do seem to recall a lot of ham being ordered up on sandwiches."

"Exactly." She butted him again, but this time she settled close, rubbing her cheek against his chest when she was done. "You're thinking on your feet. You're making decisions on the fly, using familiar skills, not ones stored in your memory banks."

"Hmm," he mused again because humming was easier than burying the truth beneath a smooth bundle of lies—lies she'd never believe anyway.

He swore then and there that no other woman had ever seen him so clearly. And then he swore for being way too pleased that she did.

So when she said, "Tripp?" in a voice that was all sugar and spice, one he knew would be matched by a dreamy soft look in her doe-bright eyes, he couldn't help it. He gave in and looked down.

And she either wasn't as frightened as she'd been claiming to be or she really thought he could save her.

Tripp sighed. It was bloody damned hell having a woman look at you like that. Like you were the hero she'd been waiting for.

He pretended that he needed to clear his throat. "Thing is, Glory, I'm not exactly an engineering project consultant."

She nodded with way too much know-it-all enthusiasm—which made her *such* an easy target to tease.

"I leap tall buildings in single bounds. I spin webs in any size. You know," he added, struggling to keep a straight face. "To catch thieves. Like they were flies."

"Dammit, Shaughnessey. I'm going to have to hurt you now."

He braced himself for the attack, nose scrunched, eyes screwed up. So he was totally unprepared for her to kiss him. And that was exactly what she did.

Her lips moved lightly over his, trembling as she murmured his name, and plea after plea to help her, to talk to her, to tell her that they'd both be okay.

He didn't have the use of his hands, goddamn it, and could only shift around until he was sitting sideways and could press her skull to the wall.

He silenced her murmurs with a bruising, punishing kiss. She had no idea what she was asking. How he had sworn never to make promises to anyone again.

But she tasted like fine spun cotton candy, like all the good things a man wanted in his life. And he knew that long-ago oath wasn't worth the air he'd written it on that first night spent on his belly crawling through Colombia's rain forest with cocaine on his fingertips and a bullet in his thigh.

He kissed her anyway, because it was better than thinking, than talking, and because she just plain knew how to kiss. So few women did, or even knew what a kiss did to a man. How nothing but the feel of soft lips and compliance could bring him to his knees.

Glory's kiss did it all, which was why he had to pull away, ease away, set her away and give her the truth. "I trained in Special Ops and spent more than a few years as a sniper."

"A sniper?" she asked, her voice low and awed. "Like with a gun?"

"No," he replied, wanting none of her awe. "With my dick."

She glared deeply into his eyes. "You, Shaughnessey, are cruisin' for a bruisin'."

"Maybe so," he admitted, lightening up the mood. "But at least I'm cruisin' faster than a speeding bullet."

She silently studied his face for a moment before she asked, "Have you killed people?"

He nodded, added, "No one who didn't deserve it."

"You're comfortable making that call?"

He'd had to be. It was kill or be killed. Kill or watch innocent victims die of bullets, of abuse, needles in their veins or powder up their nose. "Are you going to judge me now? Change your mind about dessert?"

She rocked her head side to side. "I think all I'm doing is trying to figure you out."

"That could take a fairly long lifetime. I haven't yet managed it and I've been living with myself for, uh, quite a few years."

"How many?" she asked and nearly caught him off guard.

He leaned forward, rubbed his nose over hers. "Now, sweetheart. Numbers don't matter. You're only as old as you feel."

"Since my hands aren't free at the moment to do any feeling, I need you to tell me."

"You are a clever little thing, aren't you."

"Actually, this faux cleverness is a weak attempt to keep my mind occupied." She sighed, deflated, closed her eyes for a moment, then opened them and stared across the room. "Otherwise, I'm going to think too much about what's going to happen next and whether I'm going to walk out of here alive."

"You will. We both will."

"How do you know?"

"It's what I do, remember? All that web-spinning and building-leaping?" When she looked even less convinced, he sighed. "Glory, listen to me. Even if the SOS wasn't picked up, I'll get us out of here. This is what I do. I need you to trust me."

"I do. It's just . . ."

"Just what?"

"It's just that I had an argument with my mother this morning and we didn't exactly hang up the phone on the best of terms."

God, but she was going to break his heart. Yet he went on making promises anyway. "No worries. You two can kiss and make up as soon as we're out of here."

"Do you think she and my father know what's happening?"

"With the police out front? I'm sure NewsChannel 4 is already on the scene. Plus, wanting to learn what they could about the shop . . ."

"The cops would've called my parents." She dropped her gaze, shifted so that she was leaning more against the wall than against him. "I don't want them to worry. I wish I could let them know I'm okay."

He hated that he couldn't offer her the cell phone he'd taken off the lookout. But Vuong could return any second and Tripp wasn't about to give up any advantage.

"Right now it's a standoff. No shots have been fired and no demands made."

"That we know of, anyway."

He nodded. "True. But this Danh Vuong didn't sound like a man with demands to make of anyone outside. What he wants is in here."

"That's what I don't get. I don't launder money or harbor political prisoners. What could he possibly want?"

Tripp blew out a long breath. If he told her the truth, he'd be jeopardizing his own case by exposing the Spectra agent. But he'd also have an intelligent and informed ally. And that never hurt in a pinch.

He bit the bullet. "The professor working on his memoir is not a professor. He's an agent of an international crime syndicate and he's using your shop as a drop point."

"A drop point," she echoed.

"A courier from Marian Diamonds is either being blackmailed into giving up details on illegal shipments out of Sierra Leone or is selling his soul to the devil."

"And you know this how? No, wait." She closed her eyes, shook her head. "I'm dizzy with these webs you're spinning, Tripp."

"Sorry, sweetheart. It's not a pretty life I lead. But I figure it's best you realize what you're dealing with here."

"What I'm dealing with? Are you kidding? I can't digest half of what you've said. Well, except for the part where you swore you wouldn't let anything happen to me."

"Did I say that?"

"I sure hope I didn't dream it. Though, actually, if I were

dreaming all of this it would be a whole lot easier to deal with because morning would be on the way." She settled closer again. "You know, morning? Waking up? Stretching, yawning, getting a cup of coffee?"

"What about the smooching?"

One dark brow went up. "Smooching?"

"Smooching, cuddling. All those juicy early morning wake-up goodies."

"And here I thought you were above all that physical stuff."

"Are you kidding? That physical stuff is what guys are made off."

"What happened to frogs and snails and puppy dog tails?"

"Ah, those were the days."

"Right. Now it's all about spiderwebs," she said and collapsed in on herself as if she'd exhausted her energy reserve.

Tripp had to keep her going. She'd be better able to stand up to Vuong, stay safe, stay strong, when alert. "What were you and your mother arguing about?"

Her eyes fluttered open and she laughed with a reckless hysteria. "About my choices in men."

"Oh, really." He perked up at that. "Sounds like a better way to pass the time than talking about me."

"What makes you think talking about the men in my life doesn't include you?"

"Does it?" he asked with a gulp.

"It should. Especially considering my mother's biggest complaint is that my two longest-running relationships have been with men belonging to a questionably criminal element."

"I'm crushed. Criminal element indeed."

She shrugged. "Hey, if the web fits."

He chuckled. "Funny girl."

"Do you have one, Tripp?"

"A web? A criminal element?"

"A girl."

He sighed, leaned forward to nuzzle his nose against her

temple, breathing in the sweet smell of her hair. "I'm pretty sure I do. At least I'm working on it."

"Oh, Tripp." She dusted kisses over his cheek, huddling up into the cradle of his neck and shoulder. "When we get out of here, can we work a little harder? Together? I'd really like it if we could."

"You're not just saying that because you want to swing on my web, are you?"

"No, I'm saying it because you've teased me for months. And because I didn't get the chance earlier to finish what I started."

He pretended to ponder. "That's true. That was all rather one-sided."

"Not my intention, trust me."

Talking about sex here and now seemed a bit like fiddling while the *Titanic* went down. But he was up for any distraction to keep Glory calm.

It was unfortunate Vuong had bound their hands. And damn unfortunate that Tripp himself had been the one to stash the knife.

"Well, if your intentions involve giving as good as you got, I'm all for some heavy-duty exploration of what you have on your mind."

"Giving as good as I got? You think rather highly of yourself, don't you Shaughnessey?"

"I'm just a man confident in his skills."

"Oh, I see," she said, her mouth twisting around what he was sure was a hell of a laugh at his expense. "What're you going to do if I give even better?"

"Guess I'll be up a creek and have to do a lot of extra paddling to make up for it."

"If by paddling you mean spanking, no thanks. But if by paddling you mean, well . . ."

Cute. She'd embarrassed herself into a corner. He leaned forward and kissed her on the lips, rubbing his lips over hers lightly, gently, teasingly, because he wanted her to be the one to open up and beg.

He wanted that because it was so much easier to let himself fall when he knew he wasn't falling alone.

When she opened her mouth, she opened it with a whimpering groan, bathing his lips with the barest tip of her tongue before pressing the seam where he held his mouth in a tightly determined line.

The funny thing about determination, he mused, was how quickly the reasoning behind it fell into a big black hole of need. The physical, he readily owned up to. The emotional, however, he was just beginning to understand when the storeroom door crashed open for the second time.

Nine

Glory jerked away from the bliss that was Tripp and banged the back of her head on the wall. Tripp scrambled to his feet. She wasn't quite as quick, what with not being a superhero and wearing a really short skirt.

Boy, had it seemed like a good idea at the time she'd been dressing this morning. And, boy, what she wouldn't give to turn back the clock and start this day over. She'd wear a flour sack and a chastity belt if given the magical chance.

But this was her reality, and she managed to stand just as the professor who wasn't came stumbling into the storeroom, Danh shoving him from behind.

Danh looked from Tripp to Glory to the older man who had gained his balance and now stood in the center of the room. Danh circled the professor or the agent or whoever the hell the man was, prodding him with the business end of his gun.

"Here are the rules for this party. Mr. Shaughnessey, you will sit back down."

Glory glanced at Tripp's inscrutable expression, watching his gaze never waver from Danh's, watching as he slid down the wall to sit.

"Very well done," Danh said, turning his attention to her. "Miss Brighton, you will turn around so I can cut you free."

Her heart fluttered at the thought of gaining her freedom, sank at the realization that she wasn't free at all. Simply being used as a pawn in Danh's game.

Facing Tripp, she presented Danh with her bound hands, wincing as he cut through the hard plastic tie. Blood rushed back into her wrists and fingers; she clasped her hands at her waist and rubbed at the bruises.

Tripp's face remained impossible to read. She had no idea if he wanted her to play nice, make a run for the door, maybe try to slip his knife out of the Advil box and use it.

Or, if all she needed to do was distract Danh by cooperating with whatever he had in mind while Tripp did what he had been trained to do.

In the end, the decision was taken out of her hands when Danh gave her a directive. "Now, Miss Brighton. I'm going to have you search the professor here for the information he has that belongs to my employer."

Knowing the man wasn't a professor at all but a member of a crime syndicate should've made the prospect easier to face. But, in fact, the opposite was true.

She looked up at his kindly, forgiving expression and tried to smile in return. Knowing the evil heart that beat beneath his tweed jacket and chocolate cashmere turtleneck sent her thoughts racing in directions she didn't want them to go.

The idea of the crimes he might have committed, the horrors he'd perpetrated . . . she couldn't even pry her fingers apart to touch his clothes.

"Haven't you done that already? Searched him, I mean?"

"Cursorily. I want you to be more thorough. One hundred percent thorough. And you can start by helping him remove his jacket."

Glory moved around behind the professor and lifted shaking hands to his shoulders.

"I'm so sorry about this," she whispered, speaking to the man she wished he was, speaking to herself. Even speaking to Tripp, apologizing for not knowing anything to do to help him get them out of here.

"Don't worry about it, my dear. We are all forced to deal with certain unpleasantries in our lives," he said, shrugging out of fashionable and expensive tweed.

Glory stepped back, holding the jacket by the padded shoulders, waiting for further instruction. The professor smoothed down the rumpled sleeves of his shirt.

Danh moved to face him, his gun now seeming to be an extension of his arm rather than a weapon. "Unpleasantries. An interesting turn of phrase for a man in your profession, yes?"

The professor's gray eyes studied Danh from behind wire-rimmed glasses. "I suppose were you to poll my students, they might agree."

Danh laughed at that, a tight humorless sound that left a trail as it crawled over Glory's skin "We're among friends here. Or at least among those similarly invested in leaving here unexposed."

Glory slid her gaze to Tripp's face. His eyes were focused on the professor's. And she swore she saw him give the other man a signal. All this subterfuge . . . who did he think she was that she was going to fall apart while these three cats batted around a mouse she couldn't see?

"Miss Brighton. The coat seams, collar, pockets, lining. Shred the garment if you must."

"What am I looking for?"

"Anything that doesn't belong."

"And if I don't find anything?" she asked, fingering the collar from point to point.

"Shoes or shirt next. We strip the professor bare if need be. And then we search his person."

"Wait the hell a minute. I am not taking off this man's clothes."

No sooner had she gotten the words out than she found Danh standing over Tripp and lining up his head as a target. "I think you'll do what you're instructed to do. There will be consequences if you do not."

Tears welled and burned until her vision was nothing but a blur of tweed. That blur was so much better, however, than picturing what a bullet would do to Tripp's head.

She moved to the pockets, the lapels, laying the jacket out on the floor and running her fingers over every inch of the lining as well as the heavier outer fabric. She finally stood, folding it over her arms.

She shook her head. "There's nothing here."

"Professor? Where would you like her to continue?"

"Miss Brighton," the professor addressed her directly. "I understand your concern, but please realize I am aware that you have no choice."

And you? she wanted to ask. If you're who Tripp says you are, what sort of choices do you have? "It would go easier on all of us if you could give me a hint? Or maybe just give Mr. Vuong what he's looking for, and save all of us this hassle?"

"She has a point," Tripp finally put in, Danh having removed the gun from the top of his head. "Give up the goods and we can all go home."

The professor's expression remained unaffected. Apparently he wasn't as put off by having her strip him as she was by the reality of the act. He slipped off his turtleneck with a nonchalance that was strangely disturbing and handed her the shirt.

Danh circled the both of them while she went through the same process of searching seams and hems. "Professor. Why don't you tell us about the memoir you're writing. With your experience, you must have more than a few tales to tell."

Why the hell was Danh baiting the man? Nothing good was going to come of this, Glory just knew. She found nothing embedded anywhere in the shirt and glanced helplessly at

Tripp. His response was no more than a look that encouraged her to hang in and he'd figure a way out of here soon.

"I'm not so sure this is the time and place for stories," the professor argued as he heel-toed off both shoes for Glory's inspection.

"It's time for whatever I decide. Do you have a publisher for your memoir? Do you have an audience waiting to read about your life?"

The professor's smile was a picture of paternal patience. "I'm not seeking publication, Mr. Vuong. I'm recording my memories as a self-indulgent exercise more than anything."

"Is that right? So if I have one of my men bring in your portfolio, then you will read to us?"

Glory sensed a shift in the room's tension even before she got to her feet with the shoes hooked over two of her fingers. Tripp had moved from leaning against the wall, his knees drawn up, his hands at his back, to a sitting sort of crouch as if ready to launch himself forward.

The professor, now bare-chested and barefooted, pushed his glasses farther up his nose. It seemed to Glory that he was using the motion as a cover, or else as a signal to Tripp.

She had no idea what was going on, what part in this drama she was supposed to be playing. So she simply offered Danh the shoes. "There's nothing here."

Danh never even looked at her. He gave all of his attention to the professor, gesturing the length of the other man's body with his gun. "It's your choice, Professor. Hand Miss Brighton your belt and your trousers. Or tell me what you've done with the information passed to you by the courier."

"Courier? I'm sure I don't know what it is you're talking about."

Danh swung. The gun cracked into the professor's skull above his ear. His glasses skidded across the floor and between Tripp's feet. Nobody moved. Glory watched blood trickle between the professor's fingers where he held his hand to his head.

Screw the little punk with the gun. Even if the professor was the agent Tripp said he was, the man didn't deserve this inhumane treatment.

She crossed the room and had her hand on the lid of the plastic storage crate when Danh ordered, "Stop where you are, Miss Brighton."

She mentally flipped him off, opened the crate and gathered a handful of napkins. "I will not stop. This man is bleeding."

She handed the napkins to the professor, then crossed her arms and faced Danh directly. "I'm done here. You obviously don't expect to find anything in his clothing. You're just playing some sick game, and it's got to stop."

Even as she said it, she sensed the professor removing his belt on her right, Tripp pushing up to his feet on her left. She was in deep shit, she knew it, and she no longer cared. If this was going to be her end, so be it. She just wanted this ridiculous siege of her property over with.

And then Danh began to laugh, a chuckle that was part desperation, part admiration, and a lot of disbelief. When he finally spoke, it was to call out in his language for one of his henchmen, to whom he issued orders while never breaking eye contact with her.

She ignored the professor's offering of the belt, turned to Tripp for help and mouthed, *What now?*

He cast a brief glance toward the professor, gave an even briefer nod before looking at her again and answering with a silent, *Bathroom.*

He wanted her to go to the bathroom. He wanted her out of here. She could only imagine that he had a plan and was sending her out of harm's way. She longed to go, felt she should stay. After all, she was on a roll, albeit a reckless one.

She inhaled deeply, exhaled, and hurried forward before she lost her nerve. "Mr. Vuong," was all she got out before his man had taken hold of her upper arm and started propelling her toward the door.

"What's going on? What are you doing?"

"I think you need to freshen up, Miss Brighton, and leave the business of negotiation to the men."

And that was all she heard.

Seconds later, she found herself being shoved through the door and into the women's restroom.

Ten

Glory gripped the edges of the white porcelain sink and hung her head. A part of her wanted to do nothing but break down and sob. Another part of her wasn't sure she'd ever be able to cry again, or if she'd ever have reason to.

If she couldn't come to real tears over *this,* the most horrific experience of her twenty-seven years . . .

Her eyes stung. It was impossible to blink. But still there was nothing. No reaction. Just nothing. Here she was alone, momentarily safe, yet none of the tears that had welled before would come.

She supposed the mind-racing processes of logic and reasoning had squashed all emotional response. And then she snorted. At least they could've put out some effort to answering her number one burning question.

Who the hell *was* Tripp Shaughnessey?

She'd only begun to ponder all the possibilities when she heard a quiet scratching against the ceiling tiles overhead. She brought her gaze up slowly, remained absolutely still but for her eyes that searched the mirror's reflection of the small room behind.

A ceiling tile shifted, dislodged from the frame. A second followed until there was a gaping black hole in the corner nearest the door. She froze, this time not even moving her eyes, staring as a face smeared with camouflage paint appeared in the opening.

Her heart thundered. She tried to swallow her fear but choked. Her palms grew slick with sweat against the cool porcelain sink.

The man put a silencing finger to his lips and she nodded, watching mesmerized as he vanished, then reappeared feet first, dropping to the floor behind her.

She turned around as a second man followed, indistinguishable from the first in the same camo gear. He remained silent and still as a third man appeared.

This one had black hair pulled to his nape in a ponytail. He also seemed to be in charge as he was the only one who spoke. "Are you all right?"

She nodded.

"Is anyone hurt?"

She shook her head.

He pressed his lips together as if satisfied, then asked, "Where's Tripp?"

"In the storeroom," she whispered, her biggest question answered. As if there had really been any doubt. Tripp Shaughnessey was not at all who he seemed.

"We counted six intruders. Is that right?"

She thought for a minute. "It's hard to say. I can't tell one from the next. Except for Danh and the one Tripp knocked out, they're all still wearing their masks. I haven't seen but four together at a time."

"Danh?"

"The one in charge." She swallowed. Her hands began to shake. "The one holding Tripp."

The dark-haired man nodded, turned to his friends, gestured in what looked like a series of coded signals. Both gave sharp affirmative shakes of their heads, and then the first man approached.

"I need you to follow my instructions, okay?"

As if she'd expected otherwise. "Sure."

"Lock yourself in one of the stalls and don't move until we're back."

"And if you don't come back?" she asked, because she couldn't help consider the possibility after the day she'd had.

He smiled at that. Camo paint or not, it was a look she was certain had left more than a few women speechless, a look that was all about confidence and certainty, even while it glinted with a cockiness that said she had no idea who she was dealing with.

Before today, she would've agreed. But that was before today. "Right. You'll be back. And what then?"

"First things first," he said and motioned for her to lock herself away.

She did, only reluctant because she wanted to see and hear and know what was going on. This was her shop, dammit. Her customers, her employee, her livelihood under siege. As it was, she wasn't even able to pace. The space between the toilet and stall door was nil.

She knew Tripp's three associates had left the room, though she'd never heard them go. Now all she could do was wait. She did so with her head braced against the stall door, her body flat, her hands splayed at her sides, her fingers spread. It was a silly pose, really, but it enabled her to breathe calmly instead of hyperventilate.

A thud in the hallway outside brought her head up a short time later. She laced her fingers tightly, then loosely, worrying them at her waist. Minutes passed, or seconds—she had lost all sense of time—another thud sounded, followed by a scuffle, though she never heard a single voice cry out or call orders.

She was crazy with wanting to know what was happening, insane with the realization that there was nothing she could do to help. She was locked in a toilet; it felt so wrong to pray, though she was certain her mother's First Presbyterian prayer circle would tell her a toilet was as good as any place.

And so she did, sending up wishes and hopes and supplications as best she knew how, wondering if any of the unanswered phone calls had been her father checking in, ready to give her his lecture, wondering how hurt her parents would be to know she'd fallen for another dangerous man.

Suddenly she wanted more than anything to ask about her father's meat loaf sandwich. To find out if the potato pancakes had been too salty as they usually were. She wanted to talk to her mother, to hear her scolding voice and promise to go out with any guy she wanted her to meet.

A patently untrue promise, of course, because the only man she wanted in her life was three doors away if she counted the one on the stall. Three doors and an entire lifetime of experience. The fact that he had any interest in her at all left her surprised.

She was no one but Glory Brighton, hardly interesting to a man who had seen the world, though she had to admit she did seem to attract ones followed by trouble. Yet even as she entertained the thought, she knew it wasn't true. Tripp was nothing like the troublemakers she'd known in the past.

He was all about solving problems and saving the world from men like those others. From men like the ones who had threatened all that she knew, all that she had. If she got out of here in once piece, she swore she'd pull a Scarlett O'Hara and take an oath to stand up for what was hers and to never go hungry again.

In the next moment, the bathroom door squeaked open. She spun around, pressed one eye to the crack below the stall's hinges. One by one, the three men returned. Tripp followed. She couldn't stay put any longer and slid back the flimsy lock on the door.

The moment he spread wide his arms, she was there, her face buried against his chest, her arms around his waist, his around hers. He smelled so good. He felt like her world, like he was everything she would ever want or need, and she wasn't sure she knew how to let him go. Knew as well that, for now, she had to.

"Sweetheart, are you okay?" he murmured into her hair.

"What about you?" She pulled away frowning, holding his hands and rubbing the dried blood from the skin on his wrists.

"All in a day's work."

"Your day maybe. Not mine." And upon saying that, the tears finally came. Tears of relief and exhaustion and joy that she would never go hungry again—and that Tripp would be around for her to snuggle with and argue with and make love with another day.

"I've got to go," he said with no small measure of regret. "But I'll be back for you when this is all done."

"What do I do now?" she asked as the phone again started to ring.

"You answer that and tell them you're opening the door."

"And what do I say about"—she glanced toward the hallway where through the door still propped open she saw . . . —"the bodies."

"That a man of steel spun a sticky web." He said it with a smile she wanted to return but couldn't. Not even after he lowered his head, rubbed his nose over the tip of hers, and kissed her soundly.

When he finally lifted his head, she blinked stupidly. His grin cleared her sensual fog. "No, really. What do I say?"

Tripp glanced up as his three associates vanished into the ceiling. He quickly spelled out her cover story. She absorbed it all, ran the explanation over in her mind until she was certain she had no questions.

Then she backed across the room and watched Tripp pull himself up through the gaping hole in the ceiling, disappearing behind the tiles he settled back into place.

Okay. First step. Take a deep breath. Second step. Answer the phone. A move that required she leave the restroom and circumvent the pile of bodies. She could do this. She could do this.

Eyes scrunched up, she scurried down the hallway and into the shop.

"Glory, sheesh." Neal struggled to gain his feet. "Where

have you been? What's going on? How'd you get by that son of a bitch?"

"I've got to get the phone, Neal. But come here. I'll cut you loose and you can free the others."

"They're gone?" asked the lighter-haired of the two secretaries, duct tape hanging loose from her mouth. "What happened?"

"Long story made short, they've been put out of commission." Glory said, instead of blurting out the truth of men of steel and webs.

She made but the briefest eye contact with the professor as he entered the room under his own steam to a round of gasps and questions, before she picked up the phone.

"Glory Brighton here."

Tripp showered and changed clothes in the ops center's locker room after an hour spent between the treadmill and the weights.

Julian, Christian and Kelly John had cleaned up first. They had more to clean up, what with the grease paint they'd worn to avoid recognition—the sort of disguise they rarely had to wear.

But they'd been operating on their own turf, in close proximity to the very building housing the office that was their cover. The camouflage had been about self-preservation, not about blending into the jungle of the city.

All any of them could do now was keep their fingers crossed that the strategy had worked.

Wearing nothing but a towel around his waist and another draped over his head, Tripp padded into the dressing area. Glory should be done with the police by now. At least with anything they were going to need her for tonight.

Now it was his turn to get to her and finish what they'd started. He wanted to make sure she was okay, that she wasn't alone and frightened, that she knew he hadn't lied when he'd promised to come back.

He tugged the towel from his head to find he had company.

Hank Smithson stood with his hands in his pockets and the butt end of a cigar in the corner of his mouth.

"Julian's off to Miami, but I'm taking Christian and Kelly John to dinner since they're pissin' and moanin' about never gettin' their lunch." Hank rocked back on his boot heels. "You up for a steak?"

Lunch, right. The reason he'd gone to Brighton's all those hours before. Tripp pulled his duffel out of his locker, tossed his towel to the bench behind him.

"Actually, I'm off to see a girl about a promise," he said, stepping into his boxers.

Hank nodded, shifted his cigar to the other side of his mouth. "I figured you might be thinking of something along those lines. Kinda surprised to hear you've been making promises, though."

Buttoning the fly on his jeans, Tripp glanced over with a grin. "Yeah, sorta shocked myself with that one."

"The girl's a good influence."

"She gets my jokes," Tripp said, surprising himself. "She doesn't necessarily laugh, but she gets them."

Hank stopped rocking, pulled his hands from his pockets and crossed his arms over his chest. "Maybe she knows what I know. That life doesn't have to be funny all the time. That doesn't mean it ain't worth living."

Tripp tugged a black T-shirt down over his head, sat to pull on socks and his boots. "Guess I'm pretty transparent, huh?"

"No. You just need to forgive yourself for the things no one else holds against you. The past is the past, son. You need to see to your future."

"With Glory, you mean?"

Hank turned to go. "With whoever makes you happy for all the right reasons."

Ten minutes later, Tripp stood on the sidewalk, arms crossed, hands in his pits, watching the lights of the ambulances and patrol cars flash off Brighton's front glass.

The hostages had been examined by paramedics, statements had been taken by detectives, and the scene combed by the forensics team. The media was now out in force.

He figured the patrol cars in the distance were hauling Vuong's gang away, finishing the job the SG-5 team had started. Good riddance to the lot of the bastards for the scare they'd given Glory.

A scare Tripp still felt burning like an ember he'd stepped on with bare feet. Damn, but he'd come way too close to losing her and any chance to tell her how crazy he was with wanting to get to know her.

A new burst of cameras flashing had him looking toward the door just as Glory came out flanked by two people he'd bet money were her parents. Her mother even had the same curly head of hair. A policeman in front of them staved off reporters as the three slid into the back of his car.

Good. She was on her way home with an escort who would make sure she got there. Relief swept through him; he'd had no idea he was still so tense. Or so hungry to see her again. He'd give them time, hang out for a while until they'd finished up their reunion. Then he'd make his move.

It was when he stepped back and turned to go that his world fell apart. In the crowd across the street he saw one face staring his way.

Danh Vuong.

Sonofabitch.

He must've escaped during the melee of the cops separating victims from violators. Through the alley door, most likely, though Tripp couldn't believe that entrance wouldn't have been under surveillance all afternoon.

But how he'd gotten loose from the ropes . . . double-jointed little fuck, dislocating his own shoulder while Tripp looked on, demonstrating exactly how he'd slipped his hands free.

Tripp stood immobile, watching the Asian kid, torn between charging across the street or grabbing the closest cop, knowing he could do neither without jeopardizing SG-5.

He'd have to explain how he knew Vuong. What he'd seen. How he'd gotten free. Why he'd left all the others behind.

Who the Spectra agent was and why his help had been enlisted.

As far as anyone but Glory and the agent knew, Tripp hadn't been there. He couldn't be found out. Couldn't risk exposing SG-5. Couldn't let the others go down because of his mistake.

All he could do was watch Danh Vuong disappear into the crowd.

Eleven

"Mom, I swear I'm fine," Glory said, pulling open her efficiency's front door, having assured her parents of the very same thing for the last hour over hot tea and chicken noodle soup. "All I want to do is soak in the tub for an hour and then sleep for at least twelve."

Ann Brighton stepped into the hallway, both hands tightly gripping the gold chain handle of her tiny black purse. Her curly black hair, so similar to Glory's, was threaded with the silver strands of her age. "I wish you'd reconsider and stay at the house with us. You could go to prayer circle with me in the morning."

Glory wasn't at all opposed to the idea considering today she'd used up her stored allotment of appeals to all higher powers. But right now the only place she wanted to be was in her own bed. "I'll come with you next week, okay?"

Her mother nodded, backed further into the walk-up's tiny hallway, her lips pressed tightly together as if clamping down on further concern.

Milt Brighton followed, giving his daughter a huge hug from which Glory hated to be released. She held tight to his hand until he was out of her reach.

"Your mother's right," he said, pushing his big blocky

glasses back into place, running a hand back over his shock of white hair. "We'd both feel better if you'd stay with us."

"I'll lock up tight. I've set the alarm on the windows." She shifted her weight to her other hip, cocked her head. "Besides, the break-in had nothing to do with me, and the perpetrators are locked up. I'll be fine."

"Promise you'll call if you need anything. If you just want to talk. If you want us to come back." Her mother glanced over Glory's shoulder into the apartment's main room. "We could stay now, sleep on your sofa bed."

"Mom, I'm twenty-seven years old and I've been living on my own for ten of those. I love you to death but I need to unwind here on my own."

Her dad wrapped his arm around her mother's shoulders. "You hear so much as a squeak, you call us, Glory Marie."

"I will, Dad. I promise." She kissed them both once more, then locked up and headed for the bathroom.

Ten minutes later, however, she heard a knock at her door. With her bathwater running and her feet already wet, she slipped into her robe and padded silently through the apartment.

She doubted her parents had returned, but she did not want to face curious neighbors or the insistent media. The eyes she saw, however, when she pressed one of hers to her peephole, were the only eyes she wanted to see.

Her pulse raced in a pitter-patter rhythm. Her palms grew wet enough that she wondered if she'd even be able to unlock and open the door.

Tripp knocked again, more softly this time as if he had decided she was sleeping, didn't want to wake her, was thinking of turning away . . .

She used the pocket of her bathrobe as a hand towel and managed to flip dead bolts, slide locks, and pull open the door before he'd gotten but six feet down the hall.

"Hi," she said breathlessly.

"Hi," he said, sounding winded.

"You look good for a man who's been busy saving the world," she said, her gaze taking in all of him.

He glanced down as if trying to see what she saw. "Part of the job description. Looking good inspires confidence."

"Oh. Is that it?" she asked, and he nodded.

In the quiet that followed, she heard water running. She gestured over her shoulder toward the small bathroom accessible only through her bedroom. "I was about to take a bath and need to get that before I flood my neighbor downstairs. Would you like to come in and wait?"

He stood leaning forward a bit, his hands gripping the door frame as he filled the entrance. The tense set of his jaw told her he had a lot more on his mind than checking up to see that she'd arrived home safely.

And that was okay because her thoughts of him weren't exactly about seeing to his health and well-being. "Tripp?"

His gaze narrowed in on hers. "Get the water. I'll lock the door."

She nodded but barely, because doing more than breathing suddenly seemed beyond her range of motion. Tripp Shaughnessey was in her apartment behind locked doors.

Dreams really did come true!

She scurried to the bathroom and turned off the water seconds before more than two splats of foamy white bubbles escaped the lip of the clawfoot tub and hit the floor. She slipped one arm from its sleeve, reached down to pull the plug.

She was stopped by Tripp at her back saying, "Don't."

She straightened, turned. "Don't?"

"Don't drain it. Take your bath. I'll wait."

"Okay. The place is small. You should be able to find your way back through." What a stupid thing to say when he'd found his way this far just fine.

"I thought about waiting in here."

Oh. Oh, oh. "You want to watch me bathe?"

He shrugged. "Or bathe you."

"Bathe me?" Oh. Oh, my. "Not bathe with me?"

"I showered while you were finishing up with the police," he said.

It was a hedge, not an answer. That was okay. She was nervous, too. "I saw you, you know."

"When?" he asked, his eyes sparking.

"You were on the sidewalk. When I was leaving with my parents. I thought about waving you over, but realized there would be too many explanations about me knowing you and everything."

She waited for his response, saw a multitude of ones that remained unspoken come and go in his eyes. He finally settled on looking at her with what felt like admiration, like approval, like all the things she wanted him to feel.

And then he reached back and closed the bathroom door.

"I knew there was more to you than this fabulous body," he said, reaching for the collar of her bathrobe and pushing it back, exposing her bare shoulders.

She felt the strange urge to shrug back into the warm chenille, an urge followed quickly by a polar desire to shrug it off completely.

This was what she wanted, wasn't it? To have Tripp all to herself? To explore what might be the relationship she'd been waiting for all of her life?

She let the robe fall and stood wearing fuzzy, red slouch socks, her bra and baggy sleeping boxers.

Tripp's grin spread ear to ear. "Oh, Glory. You are the most amazing woman."

Now she really wanted to grab her bathrobe off the floor and use it to cover all her imperfections and insecurities. There was nothing much amazing about her at all.

He, on the other hand . . .

He was gorgeous beyond belief. And he was looking at her as if she was truly more than he'd expected to see, to find, to discover.

The grin on his face had her nervously rubbing the toes of one sock over the Achilles' tendon of the other. And how apropos considering she was certain he would quickly become her biggest weakness.

When she took a deep shuddering breath, he stepped closer and wrapped one arm around her neck to pull her near.

She buried her face in the crook of his shoulder, absorbing his comforting warmth the way she'd so wanted to do when they'd been held captive.

He nuzzled her ear, her jaw, her throat, whispering soft nonsense about how good she smelled, how soft she was, how beautiful . . . Oh, but this felt so right. And he smelled so crisp and so clean, like a sweet apple tart.

It was when he reached back with his free hand and released the clasp of her bra that she realized they were going to go where she'd wanted to go forever. The straps slipped from her shoulders; she shifted one way then the other until the seamless white cotton fell to the floor.

Tripp set her away then, held her shoulders and her gaze for a long, tense cherry bubble bath–scented moment before he looked down.

Her nipples tightened; she drew back her shoulders, sucked in her stomach, watched his appreciative expression darken seconds before he turned them both around.

He sat on the edge of the tub, pulled her between his spread thighs, held her waist and kissed the bony spot of her sternum. She closed her eyes and swore she'd go to prayer circle with her mother every week as long as no one ever took this moment away.

"Are you okay with this?" he asked, moving side to side, kissing and nipping the plump fleshy curves of her breasts until her thighs trembled with heat.

She nodded, moved her hands to his shoulders for balance. "Oh, yeah. I'm very good with this. *You're* very good with this."

He chuckled, the sound tickling her skin. "Wait till you see what I can do with soap and a sponge."

She was going to die. No way around it. "I'm not sure I'll survive that long."

"I'll stop if you want."

She didn't want. "I'll let you know if I'm in danger of death's door."

"Taking off your socks might help."

"My socks?"

He nodded, his five o'clock shadow scraping her skin, his tongue circling around and around her nipple. "Those are deadly looking."

She smacked the back of his head. He closed his teeth over her in response. A nip, nothing more, but she groaned as the ribbon of pleasure curling through her snapped taut.

"I've had these socks since high school."

"The boxers, too?" he asked, tugging the elastic waistband lower to circle her abdomen at a spot that was dangerously low.

"Yeah. I like feeling comfortable in my things."

"How 'bout feeling comfortable out of your things?" The boxers were barely hanging on her hips by now.

"As long as you don't complain about what you see, I think I can manage a decent comfort level."

He lifted his head from her breasts, dug his thumbs into her pelvis and held her tight. His eyes, when he met her gaze, were heavy with arousal but bright with a spark of what she swore looked like anger.

"Why would you think I would have a goddamn thing to complain about?" he asked, his voice tight as he controlled his response.

"Because I'm definitely less than perfect, and that's what a lot of men seem to want."

"Perfection is in the eye of the beholder, sweetheart. And the best sex is had in the mind. Any man deserving of you would know that."

"Are you that man?"

"I'm working my way in that direction."

"Oh, Tripp," she said with a sobbing sort of sigh. "How do you manage to make me laugh and cry at the same time?"

"One of my many fine talents."

"Are you going to show me the others now?"

"Only if that's what you want."

She'd never in her life wanted anything more. And so she took a step back, brought down one heel on the toe of the opposite sock and pulled her foot free. The other sock followed in the same fashion, leaving her wearing nothing but the worn boxers. She moved her hands to her waist.

Tripp stopped her with a shake of his head. "I want to do that."

She canted her head to the side and considered him. "Okay, but first I want to see you get out of your clothes."

Twelve

Getting naked had been his plan all along, but when she put it like that . . .

He started with his feet, balancing on one to tug the boot from the opposite, reversing the process until he stood in his socks.

The room smelled like sweet cherries, and he felt like he'd fallen into a strawberry patch, what with the tiled floor of white and red and the matching curtain over the one tiny window.

Then there was Glory, standing with her arms crossed beneath her gorgeous tits, her nipples puckered like raspberries in dark chocolate centers.

He groaned at the sight, his hands going to the hem of his T-shirt, tugging it from his jeans and up over his head. He wadded it into a ball, tossed it on the floor and groaned again for what would probably be only one of a billion times tonight.

She'd shifted her weight from one hip to the other, the stretched waistband of those boxers she wore sliding farther down her body every time she moved, answering his question on their way south.

She wasn't wearing panties at all.

No bikinis, no thong, nothing. He knew that because he

could see the barest edge of the strip of dark hair above her sweet pussy lips.

"You're taking too long, Shaughnessey. The water's getting cold."

They were never going to make it into the tub at this rate anyway, so what did it matter?

He unbuttoned the fly of his jeans, shimmied them down his legs. He and Glory now both stood wearing boxers—though his were a lot tighter on his body parts than were hers.

She stepped closer, stopped when she stood at the end of his fingertips' reach, ignored what he'd said about wanting to strip her, and pushed her shorts to the floor.

He was going to come where he stood. His cock bobbed upward, his balls seized up. But it didn't take him two seconds to get as naked as she was.

Or so he thought until she pointed to his socks.

He was out of those puppies in a nanosecond, and then Glory was there, her arms around his neck, her tits flattened against his chest, her thighs open to accommodate his cock that had a heat-seeking mind of its own.

She nuzzled her nose to the side of his. "This feels so nice."

"Yeah," he squeaked out. "Nice."

She pulled back, frowned. "You don't think so?"

"Oh, Glory. If you knew what I was thinking right now . . ."

"Tell me?"

"And ruin a perfectly good fantasy?"

This time, she tilted her head to the side and, smiling, said, "Aren't I your fantasy?"

He slid his hands from where they rested in the small of her back down to cup her ass and squeeze. "All those times I've come into the shop and ordered lunch? I sure as hell wasn't thinking of eating a sandwich."

She blushed, and it was a beautiful sight, the way her cheeks colored like rosy apples. "I knew you were dying for my cake."

"I'm dying now, Glory."

"Then what are you waiting for?"

He backed her into the edge of the tub and pushed her to sit, dropping to his knees between her spread legs. Her thighs shook when he opened her wider. Her hands grew as white as the lip of the porcelain tub onto which she held.

He looked up once, saw that she'd closed her eyes, that she'd caught the edge of her bottom lip between her teeth, and so he lowered his gaze and took in the view he'd been waiting to see.

Her hair was trimmed. That he knew from touching her earlier. What he hadn't known was how dark it was against her soft skin. The lips of her pussy were plumped up, her clit hard and protruding, her juices sparkling there in her slit.

He couldn't wait. His palms on her thighs, he leaned forward and lapped, dipping the tip of his tongue into her hole, dragging the flat part up between her folds. One long, hot hard taste of her and he knew they were both in trouble here.

His cock strained toward his belly, the tip weeping. Glory shuddered until he thought she would tumble back into the tub. Water sloshed over her bottom, between her legs, onto the floor. He wet two fingers with her cream and slid them into her cunt.

She cried out, and he fucked her with his fingers, slowly, steadily, sucked at her clit with the same rhythmic motion, worked her pussy in and out and around, using lips, tongue, the crook and stroke of his fingers until she burst.

It was heat lightning, the sparks arcing between them. She contracted around his fingers, shuddered, trembled, groaned so deeply in her belly his fingers buried deep inside her body vibrated with the sound.

She was exquisite in her pleasure, and he took his time bringing her down, pulling away only when she placed a palm on his head. He got to his feet and she did the same. And then she smiled.

"My turn?" she asked, but he shook his head, scrambled for his jeans and his condoms.

"Sweetheart, as much as I'd love to tickle the back of your throat, there's something I want even more."

"Anything," she said, and he knew she would deny him nothing.

"Bend over."

She got a look in her eye that spoke of a very wicked nature and willingness to please. And then she stood on tiptoe, brushed her lips over his earlobe and whispered, "Take as much as you want."

He closed his eyes and swallowed the urge to shove himself into that mouth. "God, Glory. What are you saying?"

"Exactly what you're hearing, Tripp." And then she turned and presented him with the keys to heaven.

He used one hand to guide his cock to the mouth of her sex and shoved himself forward, waiting for the initial sensation to pass and grabbing hold of her hips for purchase.

She wiggled.

He hissed.

And then he started to move, slowly at first, soaking in her cream and the friction between them. But the temperature grew too hot too fast.

He ground his jaw and picked up the pace, slamming into her like he would take her apart. She moaned, asked for more, begged and pleaded with her mouth as well as with her cunt that gripped his cock so tightly he thought he would die.

It was over before it started. He came in a furious rush of come, unloading into her body until he was spent, drained, and on the edge of falling in love.

"Whew. I'm glad we got that out of the way."

Glory glared at the man sitting across from her in the huge tub and pelted him with her sponge. "Watch the complaints there, Shaughnessey. Or that'll be all you get out of me."

"Say it isn't so," Tripp teased, his expression that of a boy fearing he might never have a chance to snoop around the cookie jar again.

"You play nice, and we'll see how it goes." She leaned into the curve of the tub, drew her heels to her hips and stared at Tripp over the sudsy mountain of her knees. "I can't believe this day. I mean, now it's almost like it was a bad dream, but you're here, so I know it happened."

He arched a surfer blond brow. "You think I wouldn't be here if not for what happened?"

She looked at her knees instead of at him and gave a weak shrug. He tossed the sponge; it hit her square in the chest and she glared. "What was that for?"

"Because you're acting like a woman."

"I am a woman."

"I know that."

Men. Argh! "Then what are you complaining about?"

"A man can only eat so many sprouts in a week, sweetheart. I figured you might realize I was in the shop to see you."

The butterflies were back with a vengeance, and this time she had the advantage of knowing how well he knew how to take care of the tickle. "I just thought you had a thing for turkey and avocado."

He held up a finger. "Don't forget the Dijon."

"And the whole wheat."

"See? You know me as well as I know myself."

"I know what you like to eat." His ego needed no further encouragement, so she twisted her mouth a bit before admitting, "And how well you eat."

He waggled both brows. "Eating is only one of my many talents."

"What are your others?"

He studied her for several long seconds. Apparently she was more transparent than she knew, because he had no trouble seeing her probing intent.

And he wasn't too happy about it. "You're not talking about my sexual prowess, are you?"

"You have prowess?" she teased.

"I have a lot of things that might surprise you."

"I only want to know about one."

"I am a renaissance man. I do not exist in a single dimension."

"Do you carry a gun?"

That seemed to knock him back a bit. He leaned into the curve of the tub as she had, stretched out his legs until his feet straddled her hips. His knees still broke the water's surface. It was a big tub, but he was a tall man.

"I do, yes. Most of the time."

"Do you have one with you now?"

He shook his head, his mouth in a tight line as if holding in more that he wanted to say.

"What's it like? To use it?"

"I try not to."

"But you have."

He nodded again.

"Well?" She prodded with her toes beneath his thigh as well as with her words.

"It depends on the situation and the outcome, but it's never nice. I mean, I don't go out hoping I'm going to get to use it."

She remembered then that he'd been a sniper. She started to ask, held back, thinking it best to wait before dredging up his past. "Well, I never did think you were an engineer."

"Did I admit that I wasn't?"

She nodded, because what he had said was enough to convince her. "You said you spun webs and leaped tall buildings."

"Have you ever seen a blueprint? If that's not a web . . ."

"An engineer wouldn't think so."

"Hmm. Busted."

"Exactly." She waited, one second, two seconds, hoping he'd say more. When he didn't, she came right out and asked, "What do you do that requires you carry a gun? Are you FBI? CIA? DEA? Some Secret Squirrel government agent?"

"I'm pretty squirrelly, yeah."

Evasive, but cute. "You can't tell me, can you?"

"It wouldn't be a good thing for you to have to admit to your mother."

"My mother?"

"Sure." He scooted forward in the tub, grabbed her by the knees and tugged her between his spread legs. "When you take me home to meet the folks."

"And when am I going to be doing that?" she asked, so close she could see every fleck of color in his eyes.

"I'd say as soon as they start asking questions about the smile on your face."

"My smile?" God, she felt like a mynah bird.

"Yeah. The one your new boyfriend puts there."

She couldn't breathe, her heart was pounding so hard. "I have a new boyfriend?"

"You do now," he said, and covered her mouth with his.

The kiss was long and soft and sweet. He pulled her into the cradle of his body and wrapped her up in his legs. She closed hers behind his hips, felt his penis stir to life against the lips of her sex.

His hands roamed her back with the same testing pressure with which his tongue roamed her mouth. Nothing existed but the here and now for either of them. Nothing but the summer-sweet scent of the room, the warm water lapping like another tongue, the sounds of labored breathing as arousal crept in to blossom and grow.

He was hard between her legs, and she felt herself open with wanting to take him inside. He was in no hurry, however, seeming content to do no more than kiss her, make love to her with his teeth and his tongue, soft thrusts, then bolder, until he released her mouth and went to work along the line of her jaw, her neck, the curve of her ear.

She shuddered and pulled away. "You're making me crazy here, Shaughnessey."

"That's the point, sweetheart." He pulled back, looked into her eyes. "I want you on the verge of crawling out of your skin. And crawling into mine."

Thirteen

"Do you know how long I've wanted you here like this?"

Tripp stared into Glory's eyes, his throat having tightened at her softly spoken question.

They lay naked in her bed, facing each other, playing footsies while their knees touched, both resting up before they tackled cleaning the bathroom.

They'd left one hell of a wet mess on the floor.

"How long?" he finally asked, because it was a safe enough question without first admitting how long he'd wanted to be here.

"Since I'm being honest about my inner slut"—he tickled her low on her belly until she giggled—"I was mentally undressing you the first time you stood there ordering your sprouts."

"Is that so?" This time he tickled her a bit lower, until he felt her moisture seep from between her folds onto the tips of his teasing fingers.

She quivered, nodded in answer to his question, her lower lip caught between her teeth as if she were holding back a whimper or moan she didn't want him to hear.

"And here I thought all that intensity was about trying to get my order right."

"It was. I wanted to make sure you came back."

This time when he tested her wetness, he shifted his hips forward and guided the head of his cock down the seam of her pussy.

This time, he was the one who shuddered.

"Then you did your job well," he said once he'd found his voice. "I couldn't stay away."

"Because of the sandwiches?"

"No, Glory. Because of you."

"Why me?" she whispered as she wrapped exploring fingers around his shaft.

He throbbed into the vise of her hold. "Because you looked at me like you wanted me naked."

"I did not," she denied with a growl, sliding her hand the length of his cock and circling the flat of her palm over the capped head. "I purposefully looked at you like you weren't worth the time of day."

"And aren't you glad I saw right through your ruse?"

"Ha. As if."

"Well, I'm sure not a masochistic glutton for a woman's punishment."

She increased the pressure of her palm, circled the head of his cock repeatedly until he grabbed her by the waist and tumbled her on top of his body. She screeched but settled in and straddled him.

"Stop that," he grumbled. "I'd like to spend some quality time here with you, and it's not going to happen like that."

He raised his knees, and she leaned back, bracing her weight against him, her hands on her thighs, his cock nestled into the soft hair and softer skin between her legs. "Are you going to sleep here tonight?"

It was a simple question. Her tremulous tone of voice and the look in her eyes complicated his answer. He knew what he wanted, but wasn't as certain that she was ready for this to move forward as fast as it seemed to be doing.

Seemed to be, hell. As it had.

"Is that what you want?"

"Is that what you want?"

"Is there an echo in here?"

She growled again—he loved the way the sound vibrated all the way into his body—and she fell forward, catching herself with her hands planted above his shoulders. "Cruisin' for a bruisin' again, Shaughnessey? Because I am definitely in a position here to do some serious harm."

It would take him less than ten seconds to reverse their arrangement, but he loved having her above him, her wild black curls a cloud around her face, her dark cherry nipples both inches from his face.

He moved his hands from beneath his head where he'd tucked his crossed arms, cupped and kneaded her tits until her eyes glazed over and his cock bobbed between their bodies.

"Oh, Tripp, you have no idea how good that feels."

He knew exactly how good his end of the bargain felt. She was sweetly firm and her skin was softer than anything he'd ever rubbed up against. Then there was the tiny fact of how much she wanted him, the way her tongue slipped between her lips when he caught one nipple between two fingers and tugged.

"Yes. I want to spend the night. Whether or not I do is your call," he said before lifting his head and sucking the berry-ripe knot into his mouth.

"Please stay," she begged breathlessly. "In fact, if you never left it would be fine with me."

With his gut clenched and the coals in his belly stirring to life, he swirled his tongue around her, drew her into his mouth, released her to move to the playground of her other breast, but took a second or two to say, "Never's a pretty long time, sweetheart."

When he bit lightly with the barest edge of his teeth and sucked, she cried out, her neck arching as she tossed back her head.

And then she whimpered, "I know. I've never known anyone like you. I've never wanted anyone the way I want you. It's taken way too long for you to get here, Tripp, but I don't want you here if this is all you want from me."

Love at first sight was nothing he'd put much stock in. Hell, he thought, burying his face between her breasts, he wasn't sure love was anything he believed in.

What he did know and what was rapidly becoming apparent, was that he needed to be with this woman as long as she'd have him. And that what he was feeling had dived over the wall separating his comfort zone of lust and the enemy territory of involvement when she'd taken off her clothes in the bathroom.

He made his decision. He dropped his head back to the pillow, looked up into her eyes, and said, "I want to stay. I'll stay as long as you'll have me. And if all we do is cuddle up and sleep, that's fine by me."

She stared down at him, tears giving her eyes a misty sheen. The smile that lifted both corners of her mouth grabbed his heart and squeezed. "Are you just saying that to get me to put out?"

"Hell, yeah," he answered, his vision blurry, a bitch of a frog clogging his throat. "Was it that obvious?"

"It was." She shifted her weight to one arm, slid her free hand down between their bodies, wrapped her tiny cool fingers around his fire-breathing cock. "Especially since you punctuated it with this."

"Oh, well, never let it be said that I'm a master of understatement." And if she didn't let him go, let him breathe, she was going to witness the true power of his punctuation skills.

What she did, instead, was raise up onto her knees and position him exactly where he wanted to be before taking him inside and slowly sliding down into his lap.

He ground his jaw, his eyes rolling back in his head—though averting his gaze didn't do much in the way of helping him find the control she'd crushed with her very light weight.

She leaned forward, placing both palms along his rib cage and massaging her way to his shoulders. The caress was firm, not the least bit hesitant, and would've brought him to his knees if he wasn't already on his back, swaying off balance, on his way to a very big fall.

When she reversed the process, dragging her hands down

his torso, her fingertips teasing his nipples as she made her way to his navel where she threaded her fingers into the hair beneath, he couldn't help it. He surged upward, his hips leaving the mattress and taking her with him.

She fell forward, catching herself on his shoulders, one brow arched as she stared down into his eyes. "Punctuating again?"

"In bold and italics."

She chuckled, shook back her hair, then leaned down to kiss him. The spoken conversation had come to an end. Now she was talking with her tongue, teasing it over his lips, dipping it into his mouth.

And she was talking with her hips, rotating and lifting and coming back down until he was a mess of groans and hisses and sounds that had no meaning at all.

He should have been spent by now with all they'd done already, but he felt like he was fifteen, not twice that age, what with the way his cock was throbbing, his balls drawn up into his body, the entire downstairs package ready to blow.

"Glory, sweetheart. It would be really cool here if you'd stop for a second, oh, God, damn, please stop." He poured the words into her open mouth, feeling the heat of his own breath backwash over his face.

Glory stopped moving the part of her body giving him hell, but continued to kiss him, abandoning his lips to tickle his eyelids, eyebrows, his cheekbones, temples and ears, her hands kneading the balls of his shoulders all the while.

And he would've been okay. He would've calmed down and been perfectly fine. The kissing kept him mighty hard, kept him on edge without sending him over.

But as she sat there unmoving, he felt her juices begin to seep out from where their bodies joined and ease down the underside of his shaft.

And that was the end of that.

He hooked an elbow behind her neck, planted a palm in the small of her back, pulled and pressed her down while grinding their mouths and bodies together.

He pumped upward, the friction of sex against sex creating a heat that sent steam to the ceiling. He spread his raised knees, jerked his mouth from hers. She braced her forearms on his chest and curled her fingers into the muscles where his shoulders sloped down from his neck.

It was impossible not to look into her eyes. The room was dark, though she'd left a tiny lamp across the room on her desk burning; the lacy black shawl draped over the shade tossed shadowed shapes onto her skin.

But her eyes were bright with what he swore were tears burning with the same emotion making it impossible for him to speak. All he could do was move, driving, thrusting, pumping and pouring himself into her; sweat broke in the small of her back. He held her there even tighter, his hand slick with desire's perspiration.

She clenched around him then, sucking in a sharp breath as her orgasm hit. He saw that she wasn't ready, that she wanted desperately to wait, to hold on, to make what they were doing last forever.

But he was done. Her contractions were like a fist of fine fingers milking him for all he was worth. And so he gave it up, emptying himself inside her, spilling himself in ribbons of come until he had nothing left to give. Until he felt as if a blade had speared the base of his spine with a pain that was searingly sweet.

He held her tight while she came down, while she learned how to breathe evenly again. While she did her best to dry her tears on a pillowcase, her head turned so he couldn't see.

He didn't have to see. He felt the sobs she tried to suppress, but he didn't say a word. He simply held her, stroked a soothing hand down her back and told her with meaningless noises and whispered nonsense how miserable his life had been without her. How he could lie here beneath her for centuries to come and be the happiest man in the world.

They both must have dozed, because he startled awake when she disengaged their rather sticky bodies a long time later, rolling to his side and draping an arm over his chest.

"Tripp?"

"Glory?"

"Will you answer one question for me?"

"Anything."

"Why do you do what you do?"

The easiest answer of all. "Because if I don't do it, who will?"

Fourteen

Glory finally returned to Brighton's on Monday morning. The police finished their investigation over the weekend and gave her clearance to open for business again. That very business was why she had shown up two hours earlier than she usually did.

She had no idea how much cleanup she'd have to do but knew it would take longer than did her usual morning prep. She was in such a good mood, however, she didn't care how long it took or that she'd be handling most of the lunch rush—what there was of it—on her own.

Knowing it might take customers time to warm up to returning, she'd phoned Neal over the weekend and scheduled his next shift for tomorrow. The time alone didn't faze her at all. In fact, she found herself humming silly love songs and thinking of the last four nights spent with Tripp.

Cliché or not, their time together had been the best of her life. He was fun. And funny. Making her laugh about things she'd never taken the time to look at before. Like the way she never could fill an ice tray without spilling. Or how many pairs of ratty socks she actually had.

Even over the way she liked to spoon backward when they slept, tucking her knees behind his thighs and pulling his back to her chest. He said the whole point of spooning was for her to feel safe in his arms while she slept. At which point she reminded him she'd been sleeping alone for a whole lotta years, and liked the idea of being the one to offer haven to a man taking on too much of the world alone.

He'd cuddled back closer, then. Made sure they were touching everywhere possible. Which eventually led to him taking hold of her hand where it draped his waist and moving her fingers lower. The feel of his hard shaft in her palm, the soft, taut skin of his erection's head beneath her questing fingers, meant neither of them slept much at all.

Funny thing today was that she wasn't tired at all. She was too busy to be tired. So busy, in fact, that it took her a minute to register the opening and closing of the front door—until the snap of the blinds being drawn shut doused half the room's light and brought her head up.

"I'm sorry." She squinted, glanced toward the door. "I'm not quite . . . open . . . yet . . . oh . . . God . . ."

Danh Vuong headed her way, wielding a gun identical to the one he'd wielded on Thursday.

The weapon failed to deter her. She wasn't going to be a victim again. She snatched up the phone's handset and ran, punching in 9-1-1. It wasn't until she put the receiver to her ear that she realized the line was dead.

She screamed, turned back around, flung the phone at the approaching man as hard as she could. "What the hell do you want?"

He dodged the phone, but didn't stop or lower the gun. He simply walked straight up to where she stood and shoved the barrel of the weapon against the base of her throat. "It's back into the storeroom for you, Miss Brighton."

She wanted to refuse, to scratch out his eyeballs, to barrel forward and knock him over like a bowling pin. But she was rapidly losing the ability to breathe or to swallow. And so she backed her way down the hallway.

Once he'd shoved her through the door and released her, she rubbed the bruise in the hollow of her throat. "How did you get here? I saw the police take you and your gang out of here."

"You saw them take my associates," he said, one brow raised. "I managed to twist free of my bonds and hide in the same ceiling through which your rescuers arrived."

That didn't make sense. It didn't make sense. "Why didn't they look for you when they only found the five others?"

"Did you tell anyone there were six intruders? Because you were the only one who knew the truth. At least the only one who would've been around to provide the details."

Had she told the police there were six men? Had she mentioned a number?

Or had she been too busy relaying Tripp's story of how Danh's men had turned on one another? How two had disarmed the others. How their leader had taken out those who had betrayed him. How she and the professor had managed to knock him unconscious and bind them all with the zip ties they carried while they were unconscious?

Preposterous, yes. But the professor had backed her up without question. And the physical evidence supported her story. Especially since the police surveillance proved no one had gone in or out through the front, the back, or the side door into the parking garage.

"So now what?" she asked.

"Now I will stand at the front door and turn away all customers but for the one man I am waiting for."

The one from the diamond exchange. "What makes you think he'll show up?"

"Because he's been instructed to. If he does not, I will kill his family."

"You've got to be kidding me." This guy was nuts! "What could you possibly want so badly to ruin so many people's lives?"

"That is not your concern, Miss Brighton."

"But if I'm going to die because of it, I want to know."

He gestured her to back across the storeroom; he stood in

the open doorway once she had. "It is about honor, Miss Brighton. About retrieving merchandise stolen from my employer. And about paying my personal debt to him at the same time."

And then he pulled shut the door.

She paced the short room, back and forth, finally slamming her fist into the metal cabinet housing the security screen. The door sprang open, bounced against its own hinges. She watched as Danh passed beneath the camera on his way to the front door.

If only she could signal Tripp's people. But the security service had replaced the cables this morning. She shoved her fingers into her hair and tugged while she whipped around in a circle.

This wasn't happening. This couldn't be happening. Why the hell was this happening? She leaned forward, hands on her knees, to catch her breath.

When she straightened, her gaze landed on the open lip of the Advil box and Tripp's knife lying inside.

"Paperwork is the bane of a man's existence," Tripp grumbled as he filled out an expense report for Smithson Engineering, using bogus travel, entertainment and licensing receipts. He understood the company needed documentation to prove he was earning his keep.

But it was damn hard making up crap for the engineering projects on which he, uh, consulted. It meant traveling to legitimate Smithson sites and bullshitting the project managers so he'd have some clue as to what was going on if asked.

Fortunately, none of the SG-5 operatives were ever asked. Equally fortunate was the fact that none of them truly involved themselves in the construction projects or everything Smithson built would be falling to the ground.

Once Tripp had the backup organized, he printed the expense spreadsheet, attached it, and tossed the envelope across his desk with other mail needing to go out. That left him staring down at the spot where he'd been working at the information he'd dug up on Danh Vuong.

Turned out the kid was a high-ranking officer in the army of one Son Cam, a successful Vietnamese businessman with fingers in a lot of really rotten pies. His street thugs, run by kids like Vuong, handled the messier ingredients, the cleanup of the leftovers, the disposal of the trash.

Danh had been part of Cam's organization for more than half of his twenty-two years; he was younger than Tripp had thought. He'd hitched an illegal ride on a cargo ship, trading in a life of hell for a hell of a life. And right now that life seemed to be all about running Cam's diamond trade.

Tripp rubbed a hand over his forehead, then pressed the heels of both palms to both eyes. He needed to get to this kid, get him off the street, get him for what he did to Glory before he did it to anyone else.

But right now he swore he wasn't going to be getting anything done if he didn't get some sleep. He'd been kept awake for all the right reasons, but the lack of quality shut-eye was still catching up.

With the crap that had gone down at Glory's, he'd lost the Spectra agent posing as Professor Shore. It had gone against every kernel of Tripp's grain to enlist the other man's help. The Faustian bargain meant weeks of surveillance down the drain and a continuing influx of conflict diamonds into Spectra's hands.

But it had also prevented innocent lives from being lost. That, Tripp had to believe.

A hell of a weight, the choices a man made.

He shook off his exhaustion and swung his chair around, pulling up his database on Marian Diamonds. He glanced briefly at the feeds on his surveillance monitors . . .

Holy fucking crap!

He hadn't yet disconnected the Brighton feed—and a damn good thing, too. The picture of Glory's empty shop wasn't the problem; she'd told him she didn't expect her usual business today.

The static was the problem. He'd write that off to line noise if not for the fact that just then Danh Vuong walked beneath the camera.

And that the static was pulsing in an SOS.

Where the hell was Glory?

Tripp bounded from his chair, snagged his cell and his Glock, checked his clip as the safety vestibule door closed behind him. He sprinted out of the reception area and down the floor's one hallway toward the service elevator.

The elevator opened into a maze of tunnel-like hallways connecting the garage with the Smithson building and the one out of which Brighton's operated. He sprinted the length of the corridor, shoved open the outside door at the end, turned and ran down the alley toward the sandwich shop's rear entrance.

He pressed his back against the wall, gun at the ready, and reached for the door handle. Unlocked. No resistance. He glanced around, grabbed up a sheet of newsprint that had blown between his feet, and wadded it into a ball. Then he eased the door open and slipped into the shop, wedging the paper to keep the door from latching completely.

Tamping down the adrenaline pumping through his body like a rush of meth, he made his way past the men's room toward the corner and the storeroom door. He listened . . . nothing. No Glory. No Vuong. He swore he'd stepped into a crypt.

His nostrils flared as one, two, three, he turned, pressed his torso tight to the wall, peered around the corner. The vantage point gave him a clear view all the way to the store's glass front.

Vuong stood to the side of one window, watching the street traffic through a slit in the blinds.

Tripp took one silent step toward the storeroom door, eyes and gun trained on Vuong. The handle turned; he sidestepped into the room, his gaze never leaving Vuong until the door was closed.

He sensed Glory long before he swiveled to meet her gaze.

She was gorgeous, amazing, and her eyes were wide with fear. She stood in front of the security cabinet, the newly sliced coaxial cable in her hands.

God, he was crazy for this woman. This time when he mouthed, *I love you,* he meant it. And this time when she mouthed, *I love you, too,* he felt all the pieces of his life fall together.

He held up a halting hand. She nodded, mouthed, *I know. Stay put.*

He took a deep breath, positioned his weapon, slowly pulled open the door—and found himself looking down the barrel of Vuong's gun.

Fuckin' shit on a stick.

Vuong cocked his head to one side, that weird shock of dark hair tumbling onto his forehead. "Mr. Shaughnessey. Why am I not surprised to find you here?"

Tripp sensed Glory moving to stand out of sight beside the shelving unit. "Because you know I'm on your ass like white on rice."

Vuong blinked, frowned, held out his free hand. "Give me your gun."

"I don't think so," Tripp said, mentally scrambling. No one knew where he was. There'd be no backup, no camouflaged cavalry.

Vuong pushed forward into the room, fired off a round above Tripp's shoulder. He flinched, Glory whimpered, but the sound was so soft he was certain Vuong hadn't heard. Was certain the only reason he had was because she was his.

"Give me the gun, Mr. Shaughnessey."

"Not this time, Vuong." A flash of silver glinted in Tripp's peripheral vision.

"Then I'm afraid I have no choice but to kill you."

"You have every choice in the world," Tripp said, sweat running between his shoulder blades. "You're taking the easy way out."

"Easy? You think killing is easy?"

Vuong's response was not what Tripp expected, but was a hot button he would now push because nothing would convince him this man had a conscience. "Sure it is. All you have to do is squeeze the trigger."

Vuong laughed, a dangerously manic sound that echoed like shards of glass falling on the concrete floor. "If you think there is nothing more to killing, then you're not the man I thought you were."

"And if you think there is, then neither are you."

The two men stood face-to-face, guns aimed at one another's chests, chests that rose and fell with their audible breathing. The vein in Vuong's temple looked ready to explode. Time was running out. Tripp felt the spinning second hand in his gut winding down.

All it would take would be one bullet. One twitch of his trigger finger. One decision made in the blink of an eye. He could do it one more time, kill one more man. This was what he'd been trained to do. What he'd done in the jungles of Colombia so many times, he'd lost count.

He saw Glory raise the knife before he could think of the words to stop her. She lunged, hands clasped overhead, swinging down in an arc, burying the blade to the hilt in the slope of Vuong's shoulder.

His eyes shot wide, he twisted. Tripp brought his wrist down on Vuong's gun hand, his knee up on the elbow.

Crack!

Vuong went down in writhing silence. The gun spun across the room, hit the far wall, and went off. Glory screamed and ducked. Tripp jumped back, his pulse exploding, staring down at the gaping chasm where the kid's neck had been. *Jesus!* Blood pooled on the floor, Vuong's expression an agonizing death mask that softened into an eerie childlike face.

Tripp stepped over the downed man and did the only thing that mattered right now. He took Glory in his arms and squeezed until even he wasn't able to breathe, guiding her from the room, pulling the door closed behind him.

He didn't stop until they were standing embraced in the

center of the shop. He'd call the cops in a minute. Or two. Or three. When he could think to explain what had happened. When he could think beyond the fact that Glory was safe.

"Amazing, amazing, amazing." It was all he could say, his voice hoarse and ragged, his throat closing around a ball of emotion the likes of which he swore he would never survive.

"Did you mean it this time?" she whispered into his shirt, tears wetting him, her heartbeat synced with his. "About loving me?"

"Oh, goddamn yes, I meant it. I am out of my mind over you." There. He'd said it. And he'd gotten it out around that damn frog squatting in his throat.

"Oh, Tripp." Her arms tightened further where she'd wrapped up his waist. "I couldn't stay put. I just couldn't."

"Shh, sweetheart. You did good. You did just fine."

She sniffed. "For a girl without super powers, you mean?"

"Oh, Glory." He tucked her head beneath his chin, cupped the back of her head and held her. He couldn't manage another word. He could barely breathe. He stared at the clock on the wall, at the second hand ticking its way the length of the pickle and back.

"You don't need super powers. You have me." Then he closed his eyes and mind to everything but Glory. "And I have you."

*Meet the men of the Smithson Group—five spies whose best
work is done in the field and between the sheets. Smart, built,
trained to do everything well—and that's everything—they're
the guys you want on your side of the bed. Go deep undercover? No problem. Take out the bad guys? Done. Play by
the rules? I don't think so. Indulge a woman's every fantasy?
Happy to please, ma'am.
Fall in love? Hey, even a secret agent's got his weak spots . . .*

Bad boys. Good spies. Unforgettable lovers.

Episode One:
THE BANE AFFAIR
by
Alison Kent

"Smart, funny, exciting, touching, and *hot*."—Cherry Adair

"Fast, dangerous, sexy."—Shannon McKenna

Get started with Christian Bane, SG–5

Christian Bane is a man of few words, so when he talks, people listen. One of the Smithson Group's elite force, Christian's
also the walking wounded, haunted by his past. Something
about being betrayed by a woman, then left to die in a Thai
prison by the notorious crime syndicate Spectra IT gives a
guy demons. But now, Spectra has made a secret deal with a
top scientist to crack a governmental encryption technology,
and Christian has his orders: Pose as Spectra boss Peter
Deacon. Going deep undercover as the slick womanizer will
be tough for Christian. Getting cozy with the scientist's beautiful goddaughter, Natasha, to get information won't be. But

the closer he gets to Natasha, the harder it gets to deceive her. She's so alluring, so trusting, so completely unexpected he suspects someone's been giving out faulty intel. If Natasha isn't the criminal he was led to believe, they're both being played for fools. Now, with Spectra closing in, Christian's best chance for survival is to confront his demons and trust the only one he can . . . Natasha . . .

Available from Brava in October 2004.

Episode Two:
THE SHAUGHNESSEY ACCORD
by
Alison Kent

Get hot and bothered with Tripp Shaughnessey, SG–5

When someone screams Tripp Shaughnessey's name, it's usually a woman in the throes of passion or one who's just caught him with his hand in the proverbial cookie jar. Sometimes it's both. Tripp is sarcastic, fun-loving, and funny, with a habit of seducing every woman he says hello to. But the one who really gets him hot and bothered is Glory Brighton, the curvaceous owner of his favorite sandwich shop. The nonstop banter between Glory and Tripp has been leading up to a full-body kiss in the back storeroom. And that's just where they are when all hell breaks loose. Glory's past includes some very bad men connected to Spectra, men convinced she may have important intel hidden in her place. Now, with the shop under siege, and gunmen holding customers hostage, Tripp shows Glory his true colors: He's no sweet, rumpled "engineer" from the Smithson Group, but a well-trained, hard-core covert op whose easygoing rep is about to be put to the test . . .

Available from Brava in November 2004.

Episode Three:
THE SAMMS AGENDA
by
Alison Kent

Get down and dirty with Julian Samms, SG–5

From his piercing blue eyes to his commanding presence,
everything about Julian Samms says all-business and no bull.
He expects a lot from his team—some say too much. But
that's how you keep people alive, by running things smooth,
clean, and quick. Under Julian's watch, that's how it plays.
Except today. The mission was straightforward: Extract
Katrina Flurry, ex-girlfriend of deposed Spectra frontman
Peter Deacon, from her Miami condo before a hit man can
silence her for good. But things didn't go according to plan,
and Julian's suddenly on the run with a woman who gives
new meaning to high maintenance. Stuck in a cheap motel
with a force of nature who seems determined to get them
killed, Julian can't believe his luck. Katrina is infuriating, un-
predictable, adorable, and possibly the most exciting, sexy
woman he's ever met. A woman who makes Julian want to
forget his playbook and go wild, spending hours in bed. And
on the off-chance that they don't get out alive, Julian's new
live-for-today motto is starting right now . . .

Available from Brava in December 2004.

Episode Four:
THE BEACH ALIBI
by
Alison Kent

Get deep undercover with Kelly John Beach, SG–5

Kelly John Beach is a go-to guy known for covering all the bases and moving in the shadows like a ghost. But now, the ultimate spy is in big trouble: during his last mission, he was caught breaking into a Spectra IT high-rise on one of their video surveillance cameras. The SG–5 team has to make an alternate tape fast, one that proves K.J. was elsewhere at the time of the break-in. The plan is simple: Someone from Smithson will pose as K.J.'s lover, and SG–5's strategically placed cameras will record their every intimate, erotic encounter in elevators, restaurant hallways, and other daring forums. But Kelly John never expects that "alibi" to come in the form of Emma Webster, the sexy coworker who has starred in so many of his not-for-prime-time fantasies. Getting his hands—and anything else he can—on Emma under the guise of work is a dream come true. Deceiving the good-hearted, trusting woman isn't. And when Spectra realizes that the way to K.J. is through Emma, the spy is ready to come in from the cold, and show her how far he'll go to protect the woman he loves . . .

Available from Brava in January 2005.

Episode Five:
THE MCKENZIE ARTIFACT
by
Alison Kent

Get what you came for with Eli McKenzie, SG–5

Five months ago, SG–5 operative Eli McKenzie was in deep cover in Mexico, infiltrating a Spectra ring that kidnaps young girls and sells them into a life beyond imagining. Not being able to move on the Spectra scum right away was torture for the tough-but-compassionate superspy. But that wasn't the only problem—someone on the inside was slowly poisoning Eli, clouding his judgment and forcing him to make an abrupt trip back to the Smithson Group's headquarters to heal. Now, Eli's ready to return . . . with a vengeance. It seems his quick departure left a private investigator named Stella Banks in some hot water. Spectra operatives have nabbed the nosy Stella and are awaiting word on how to handle her disposal. Eli knows the only way to save her life and his is to reveal himself to Stella and get her to trust him. Seeing the way Stella takes care of the frightened girls melts Eli's armor, and soon, they find that the best way to survive this brutal assignment is to steal time in each other's arms. It's a bliss Eli's intent on keeping, no matter what he has to do to protect it. Because Eli McKenzie has unfinished business with Spectra— and with the woman who has renewed his heart—this is one man who always finishes what he starts . . .

Available from Brava in February 2005.

Please sample other books
in this wonderful series:
Available right now—
THE BANE AFFAIR

Christian watched the road rush by beneath the car, the roar in his ears much more than that of the engine or the tires. He should have trusted his instincts earlier. Susan turning green wasn't about the amount of alcohol left in her system at all.

He held out his right hand, gripped the steering wheel with his left. "Hand me your phone."

"Why?"

"The phone, Natasha." He didn't have time to argue. Didn't have time to explain. Had time to do nothing but react. An exit loomed to the right. He downshifted to slow the car and swerved across two lanes to take it. Ahead and behind, the road was blessedly free of traffic. "The phone, now, please."

"I don't think so," she said, yelping when he reached across and grabbed it out of her hand.

She slumped defiantly into her seat, arms crossed over her chest. Checking again for oncoming vehicles, he pried open the phone and removed the battery, tossed the case over the top of the car toward the ditch, the power supply to the side of the road a quarter mile away.

"What the hell are you doing?" she screamed, whirling on him, fists flying, nails raking, grabbing for the steering wheel.

He hit the brakes, whipped into the skid. The fast stop and shoulder strap slammed her back into the bucket. He kept her there with the barrel of the Ruger .45-caliber he snatched from beneath his seat. "Sit down. Nothing's going to happen to you if you sit down and be still."

She didn't say a word, but he heard her hyperventilating panic above the roar in his ears.

"Calm down. Natasha. Listen to me. No one's going to get hurt." His pulse pounded. His mind whirred. "I just need you to be still and be quiet."

"You're pointing a gun at me and you want me to be still and be quiet? You fucking piece of shit." She swiped back the hair from her face. "Don't tell me to be still and be quiet. In fact, don't tell me anything at all. When Susan doesn't hear from me later, she's calling the cops. She knows exactly where we are and what we're driving. So whatever the hell you think you're doing here, you're not getting away with it. You lying, fucking bastard."

He caught her gaze, saw the glassy fear, the damp tears she wouldn't shed, the delineated vessels in the whites of her eyes like a road map penned in red. He wanted to tell her the truth, that he was one of the good guys, to reassure her that she could trust him, that no harm would come her way—but he couldn't tell her any of that and he refused to compound his sins with yet another lie.

And so he issued a growling order. "Shut the hell up, Natasha. Now."

Grabbing his phone from his belt, he punched in a preset code. The phone rang once. Julian Samms picked up the other end. "Shoot."

"I need to get to the farm. Where's Briggs?"

"Hang," Julian ordered, and Christian waited while his SG-5 partner contacted Hank's chopper pilot, waited and watched Natasha hug herself with shaking hands, tears finally and silently rolling down her cheeks.

"I've got you on GPS. Briggs can be there in thirty, but you need to bank the car. And he needs a place to land. Hang."

More waiting. More looking for approaching cars. More watching Natasha glare, shake, and cry.

Christian switched from handset to earphone and lowered the gun to his thigh, keeping his gaze on Natasha while waiting for Julian's instructions. She seemed so small, so wounded, and he kicked himself all over again for failing to make it clear that their involvement was purely physical.

He should have spelled that out from day one, made it more clear that Peter Deacon took trophies, not lovers. But he'd never given her any such warning. Not that it would've done any good. Hell, he knew the lay of the land and here he was, so tied up in knots over what he was putting her through that he couldn't even think straight.

"My name is Christian Bane," he finally said, owing her that much. "That's all I can tell you right now."

She snorted, flipped him the bird, and turned to stare out her window.

"Bane."

"Yeah." Hand to his earpiece, he turned his attention back to Julian.

"Two miles ahead on the right," Julian said as Christian shifted into gear and accelerated, "there's a cutoff. Through a gate. Looks like a dirt road, rutted as hell."

He brought the car up to speed, scanned the landscape. "Got it," he said, and made the turn, nearly bottoming out on the first bump.

"Half a mile, make another right. Other side of a stand of trees."

"Almost there." He reached the cutoff and turned again, caught sight of the tumble down barn and stables, the flat pasture beyond. Perfect. Plenty of room for the chopper and cover for the car. "Tell Briggs we're waiting."

A short couple of seconds, and Julian said, "He says make it twenty. K.J.'s with him. He'll bring back the car. I'll keep the line open. Hank's expecting you."

"Thanks, J."

Christian maneuvered the Ferrari down the road that wasn't

much more than a trail of flattened grass leading to a clearing surrounding the barn. Once he'd circled behind it, he tugged the wire from his ear, cut the engine, and pocketed the keys. When he opened his door, Natasha finally looked over.

"Going someplace?" she asked snidely.

"We both are," he bit back. "Get out."

"You can go to hell, but I'm not going anywhere."

"Actually, you are. And you're going with me." He reminded her that he was the one with the gun.

She got out of the car, slammed the door, and was off like a rocket back down the road. Shit, shit, shit. He checked the safety, shoved the Ruger into his waistband next to the SIG, and took off after her. She was fast, but he was faster. He closed in, but she never slowed, leaving him no choice.

He grabbed her arm. She spun toward him. He took her to the ground, bracing himself for the blow. He landed hard on his shoulder, doing what he could to cushion her fall. She grunted at the impact, and he rolled on top of her, pinning her to the ground with his weight and his strength.

Her adrenaline made for a formidable foe. She shoved at his chest, pummeled him with her fists when he refused to move. He finally had no choice but to grab her wrists, stretch out her arms above her head, hold her there.

Rocks and dirt and twigs bit into his fingers. He knew she felt the bite in the backs of her hands, but still he straddled her, capturing her legs between his.

"You want to wait like this? Twenty minutes? Because we can." His chest heaved in sync with the rapid rise and fall of hers. "Or we can get up and wait at the car. I'm good either way. You tell me."

"Get off me." She spat out the words.

He rolled up and away, kept his hands on her wrists and pulled her to her feet. Then he tugged her close, making sure he had her full attention, ignoring the stabbing pain in his shoulder that didn't hurt half as much as the one in his gut. "I'm not going to put up with any shit here, Natasha. Both of our lives are very likely in danger."

"Oh, right. I can see that. You being the one with the gun and all." She jerked her hands from his.

He let her go, walking a few feet behind her as she made her way slowly back to the barn and the parked car. She had nowhere to run; hopefully, he'd made his point. He had no intention to harm her, no *reason* to harm her, but he needed to finish this job, to make sure Spectra didn't get their hands on whatever it was Bow had to sell.

And now that he'd been stupid enough to get his cover blown . . .

"Where are you taking me?" She splayed shaking palms over the Ferrari's engine bay, staring down at her skin, which was ghostly pale against the car's black sheen.

"To get the answers you've been asking for," he said, guilt eating him from the inside out, and looked up with no small bit of relief at the *thwup-thwup-thwup* of an approaching chopper.

And coming soon from Brava—

THE SAMMS AGENDA

South Miami, Friday, 3:30 P.M.

Julian hit the ground with a jolt, seams ripping, bones crunching, joints popping as he rolled to his feet and came up in a full throttle run.

Coattails flying, he sprinted across the pool's cement deck, hurdled the shattered planter, and gave Katrina no chance to do more than gasp as he grabbed her upper arm and ran.

"Go! Go! Go! Go! Go!"

He propelled her forward, knowing he could run a hell of a lot faster than she could, the both of them dragged down even more by the *slap, slap, slap* of her ridiculous shoes. She seemed to reach the very same conclusion at the very same time, however, and kicked off the slides to run barefoot.

Once across the deck and up the courtyard stairs, he shoved open the enclosure's gate. Another bullet ricocheted off the iron railing. Katrina screamed, but kept up as they pushed through and barreled down the arched walkway toward the parking garage.

Her Lexus was closer, but he doubted she had her keys. Even breaking in, hot wiring would take longer than the additional burst of speed and extra twenty-five yards they'd need to reach his Benz.

"My car. Let's go," he ordered. She followed, yelping once, cursing once, yet sticking with him all the way.

A shot cracked the pavement to the right of their path, a clean shot straight between two of the garage's support beams. Way too close for comfort. Rivers's practice was about to make perfect in ways Julian didn't want to consider.

The keyless transponder in his pocket activated the entry into his car from three feet away. He touched the handle, jerked open the SL500's driver's side door.

Katrina scrambled across the console; he slid down into his seat, punched the ignition button, shoved the transmission into reverse.

Tires screaming, he whipped backward out of the parking place and shot down the long row of cars. He hit the street in reverse, braked, spun, shifted into first, and floored it, high octane adrenaline fueling his flight.

Halfway down Grand, several near misses and an equal number of traffic violations later, he cast a quick sideways glance at Katrina and nodded. "You might want to buckle up."

She cackled like a witch. "You're suggesting that now?"

He shrugged, keeping an eye on his rearview and any unwanted company, whether Rivers or the cops. He wasn't about to stop for either. "Better late than never."

That earned him a snort, but she did as she'd been told. Then she shifted her left foot into her lap, giving him an eyeful of a whole lotta tanned and toned thigh. "I've got glass in my foot."

He didn't say anything. He had to get out of her neighborhood and ditch his car—a reality that seriously grated. "Stitches?"

She shook her head, leaning down for a closer look at the damage. "Tweezers, antibiotic ointment, and a bandage will suffice."

"I've got a first aid kit in the trunk." How many times had he patched himself up on the fly? "I'll grab it as soon as we stop. In the meantime . . ." He pulled his handkerchief from his pocket.

"Thanks." She halved it into a triangle and wrapped her foot securely, knotting the fabric on top at the base of her toes. "When you hit 95, head south. The police station's on Sunset."

He nodded, turned north at the next intersection.

"Uh, hello? I said Sunset. South, not north."

"I heard you." This wasn't the time for a long explanation as to why he couldn't go to the police, why SG-5 couldn't risk exposure, why he'd learned a long time ago that actions spoke a hell of a lot louder than words.

"Look. I appreciate the save, even if I was dumb as a stick to get in this car not knowing who you are. But we're going to the police, or I'll be making a scene like you wouldn't believe."

Oh, he believed Miss High Maintenance capable of just that. So far the only surprise had been her lack of complaints over their full-out, hundred-yard dash and the injury she'd sustained in the process.

"This isn't a police matter." Still, heading in the direction of the station might keep Rivers at bay and give Julian time to consider his options.

"And why would that be?" she asked, her incredulous tone of voice unable to mask the sound of the gears whirring in her mind. "You're with the shooter, aren't you? This kidnapping was the goal all along. You son of a bitch."

Julian couldn't help it. He smiled. It was something he rarely did and the twitch of facial muscles felt strange.

But there was just something about a woman with a potty mouth that grabbed hold of his gut and twisted him up with the possibilities. He hadn't had a really good mouth in a very long time.

A thought that sobered him right up. "No. I'm not with the shooter. His name is Benny Rivers. He's with Spectra IT and he's in Miami to take you out."

Here's a preview of

THE BEACH ALIBI

He couldn't believe it.

He *abso-fucking-lutely* couldn't believe this was happening. Not here. Not now.

He'd prepped for this mission for weeks. He knew every way into this building, every way out. Windows, elevators, ducts, doors, all of it.

How the hell could he have missed the goddamn camera hidden in the wall clock?

Kelly John Beach averted his head, stared at his shoes, at the pine green-and-navy leaf pattern in the executive suite's carpet beneath, ordered himself to think, think, *think*.

The camera was new. He hadn't missed it. The clock hadn't been here before tonight. He'd scanned this office an hour after the cleaning crew had left, doing an electronic sweep while in uniform as building security.

There had been nothing, *nothing*, on that wall other than the CFO's flat panel television.

That didn't change the fact that now there was. Or the fact that the position he was in was more than compromising.

It was neck-in-the noose illegal.

The CD of classified Spectra IT intel he'd come for was tucked safely into the vest strapped to his chest. Getting out of here wasn't going to be a problem. He'd simply reverse the trip he'd made coming in.

The trouble would come later.

Three minutes from now, he'd be ground level wearing street clothes. Give the cops another thirty, he'd be wearing handcuffs.

God-fucking-damn.

Sweat beaded on his forehead, rolled like Niagara down his spine. His eyeballs burned. His temples throbbed. His heart was a fist-size red rubber ball clogging the base of his throat.

He had to get to the SG-5 ops center without hitting the street. The only way to do that was the subway at the Broad Street station. Then underground.

He hated going underground. He hated the dark. Hated the rats. Hated the stench of shit and decay and all the rotten crap he'd have to step in.

Right, he growled, grumbled, snorted. Now he was really looking forward to the trip. But a man had to do what a man had to do, or so went the saying.

And so he did. Sucked it up, swallowed his own bullshit and the red rubber ball, and walked out of the Spectra IT office like the fucking President of the U.S. of A.

"Slow it down, son. Slow it down." Hank Smithson gestured toward Kelly John with the stub end of a cigar tucked in the crook of his index finger. "You're not going to get this figured out by wearing a hole in the floor."

The older man could use his calming techniques all he wanted. Kelly John wasn't in any mood to be calmed or gentled or put out to pasture. Not when it looked like he was about to be put down.

He paced the SG-5 ops center's huge horseshoe workstation from his own desk to Tripp Shaughnessey's and back. Again and again and again.

"Easy for you to say." He stopped, sniffed. Christ, but he smelled like a freakin' sewer. "You aren't the one who screwed up."

It was more than screwing up the mission and giving

Spectra the upper hand. It was letting down the others, exposing the Smithson Group.

Failing Hank.

Hank crossed his arms over his chest and rocked back on
his boot heels. "Kelly, you did your best."

His best hadn't been good enough. Not this time. A hell of
a hard pill to swallow considering the reason Hank had picked
him to join the Smithson Group in the first place. "They had
to know I was coming. That's the only way the timing of that
camera install makes sense."

"They were protecting their assets," Hank reminded him.

A reminder that pissed him off even further when he
thought of the source of the organization's millions. "Yeah, well,
now they've got video proving how insecure they really are.
And how stupid I really am."

Hank moved, blocking Kelly John's path, commanding his
attention. "We'll figure it out, son. We'll figure it out."

"What's to figure?"

At Tripp Shaughnessey's offhanded question, both men
turned, Kelly John glaring down at his partner where Tripp sat
on the floor in front of his desk. "What the hell's that supposed to mean?"

Tightening the wheels on his upended chair, Tripp shrugged.
"You're the computer whiz. Make your own video. Prove you
were elsewhere at the time. Show them they only think they
know what they're seeing."

"An alibi," Hank said.

Intrigued, Kelly John started pacing again. "That might
work."

"And we all know who would make the best alibi, right?"
Tripp asked.

Something in Tripp's tone told Kelly John he wasn't going
to like the answer. "Who?"

"A woman."

And here's a peek at

THE McKENZIE ARTIFACT

The drapes over his motel room's window pulled open, Eli McKenzie stood and stared through the mottled glass, squinting at the starburst shards of sunlight reflected off the windshields of the cars barreling down Highway 90 in the distance.

Second floor up meant he could see Del Rio, Texas, on the horizon, and to his left a silvery sliver of the twisting Rio Grande, a snake reminding him of the venom he'd be facing once he harnessed the guts to cross.

The room's cooling unit blew tepid air up his bare torso, making a weak attempt at drying the persistent sheet of sweat. Sweat having less to do with the heat of the day than with the choking memory of the poison he'd unknowingly ingested on his last trip here.

An accidental ingestion. A purposeful poisoning.

Someone in Mexico wanted him dead.

The only surprise there was that no one but Rabbit knew Eli's true identity. Wanting to dispose of an SG-5 operative was one thing, but he hadn't been made. Which meant this was personal.

This was about his covert identity, his posing as a member of the Spectra IT security team guarding the compound across the border.

An identity he'd lived and breathed for six months until the nausea and dysarthria, the diarrhea, ataxia and tremors turned him into a monster. One everyone around him wanted to kill.

He'd tried himself. Once.

Rabbit had stopped him and sent him back to New York and to Hank Smithson, the Smithson Group principal, to heal. Eli owed both men his life, though it was his debt to Hank that weighed heaviest.

Hank, who plucked men in need of redemption off their personal highways to hell and set them down on roads less traveled. Roads that took the SG-5 operatives places not a one of them wished to see again after reaching the end of their missions.

Places like the Spectra IT compound in Mexico.

Scratching the center of his chest, Eli shook his head and pondered his immediate future. He and Rabbit were the only ones inside the compound not working for Spectra. Outside was a different story.

And there had been one person nosing around and causing enough scenes to make a movie.

Stella Banks.

Stella Banks with her platinum blonde hair and battered straw cowboy hat and legs longer than split rail fence posts. She was an enigma. A private investigator who dressed like a barrel racer and looked like a runway model.

She kept an office in Ciudad Acuna, another in Del Rio. He knew she was working the disappearance of her office manager's daughter, Carmen Garcia. The girl was fourteen, and like so many of the others gone missing recently, a beauty.

She was also currently being held inside the compound, waiting to be shipped away from her family and into a life of prostitution courtesy of Spectra IT. Or so had been the case last Eli had checked in with Rabbit.

The room wasn't getting any cooler, the day any longer, the truth of what lay ahead any easier to swallow. Like it or not, it was time to go. Once across the border, he'd make his way

south a hundred kilometers in the heap Rabbit had left parked in a field west of the city.

As much as Eli longed for a haircut and a shave, he wouldn't bother with either. The scruffy disguise went a long way to helping him blend in, to hiding the disgust he never quite wiped from his face.

Considering the condition of the car and the roads, he was looking at a good two hours of travel time. One hundred and twenty minutes to go over the plans he'd worked out with Rabbit to take down these bastards.

Plans trickier than Eli liked to deal with but which couldn't be helped. Not with the lives of twenty teenaged girls on the line.

His plans for Stella Banks he hadn't quite nailed down.

He needed her out of the way.

Before he got rid of her, however, he needed to find out what she and her outside sources could add to what Rabbit had learned on the inside.

Only then would Eli make certain she never interfered in his mission again.

He was alive.

And he was back.

That son-of-a-bitch was back.

Stella Banks curled her fingers through the chain links of the fenced enclosure and watched him leave the compound's security office and cross the yard to the barracks.

She couldn't believe it. Not after all the trouble she'd gone through—and gotten into—to get rid of his sorry kidnapping ass for good.

Next time she'd forgo the poison and use a bullet instead.